PRINCE of UNDERWHERE

by BRUCE HALE

illustrated by
SHANE HILLMAN

PRINCE of UNDERWHERE

HarperCollins*Publishers*

Library of Congress Cataloging-in-Publication Data

Hale, Bruce.

Prince of Underwhere / by Bruce Hale ; illustrated by Shane Hillman.— 1st ed.

p.   cm. — (Underwhere ; #1)

Summary: When Zeke, his twin sister Stephanie, their neighbor Hector, and Hector's cat Fitz slide into the world of Underwhere, Zeke is hailed as a prince who will, according to an ancient prophecy, free the Undies from the evil UnderLord's rule by finding and destroying his throne.

ISBN 978-0-06-085124-8 (trade bdg.)

ISBN 978-0-06-085125-5 (lib. bdg.)

[1. Adventure and adventurers—Fiction. 2. Heroes—Fiction. 3. Magic—Fiction. 4. Cats—Fiction. 5. Brothers and sisters—Fiction. 6. Twins—Fiction. 7. Humorous stories.] I. Hillman, Shane, ill. II. Title.

PZ7.H1295Pri 2008   2007009135

[Fic]—dc22   CIP

                                                                                                    AC

Typography by Jennifer Heuer

1 2 3 4 5 6 7 8 9 10

❖

First edition

To Billy the Kid—
still crazy after
all these years

—B.H.

My Freaky Neighborhood

If we hadn't run from the spies, I might never have discovered Underwhere. (The place, not the tighty-whities. I already know about those.) Then I would never have had to walk like a zombie, lead a midget revolution, and cut a mighty cheese in a castle. Which would mean, of course, I wouldn't be battling the evil billionaire rapper and his mutant dinosaurs.

But we did, and I did, and I am, so why complain? World-saving is a lot more fun than homework, anyway.

But I'm getting ahead of myself. Let's back up.

The whole thing started because of a scruffy, stinky, good-for-nothing cat.

I was walking home from school with my twin sister, Stephanie, and our neighbor Hector. That's normal enough.

Steph and I were arguing. Also normal.

(We're not the kind of twins who think alike and act alike. Some people don't believe we're part of the same family. In fact, I'm not totally sure she's from the same planet.)

"No way, dwarf," she said. "If you use Great-aunt Zenobia in that report, I'll cream you."

"You and what blender?" I said. "You're just ticked 'cause you didn't think of it first, frizzball."

Her mouth fell open. "But I *did*! You heard me talking to Heather about it."

"Nope."

"And you ran straight to Mrs. Ricotta and told

her it was *your* idea."

"Did not."

Well, maybe I did. But no way would I admit it to her.

Hector looked across me at Steph. "Don't worry," he said. "You'll think of something. You're the smart one."

That's Hector, my best buddy. Loyal, huh?

"That's not the point," she said. "It was my idea. I should do it."

But you could tell she liked being called the smart one.

"I'm not dumb—just lazy," I said.

And that's the truth. Sort of. Look, it's not easy being twins with a megabrain like my sister. So why raise everybody's expectations? Why not let *her* be the overbusy beaver?

Steph tossed her dirt-brown curls. I think she thinks this makes her as pretty as the lady in the

Chichi shampoo commercial. *Yeesh.* In her *dreams.*

"Hey," said Hector. "Did your clocks get all wacky this morning?"

"Yeah," I said. "They wore clown noses and purple socks." That's me: I'm the funny one.

Hector ignored me. "Ours showed all different times. I was so late for school, my grandma had to drive me."

"Oh, *that* wackiness," I said.

We turned the corner onto our street.

"Same thing at our house," said Stephanie. "If I hadn't set my watch, we would've overslept."

That's Steph: so in love with school, she uses two alarms to wake her up on time. She's definitely from another planet.

"Mrrow mrow, *meer* rowww."

Hector's scraggly orange cat, Fitz, stepped from the bushes. He was carrying a lizard.

"Hey, Fitzie," said Steph. She scratched him behind the ears. "Does kittycat want to be petted?"

Fitz dropped the mangled lizard at her feet.

"Gross!" said Steph, stepping back.

"Gross!" said Hector and I, leaning in.

Fitz stared up at us with golden eyes, then back to the reptile. "Murr mrrow, meer?"

"Snack time," I said. "Want a bite, Steph?"

"It looks like . . . ," she said.

"What?" We both bent closer.

"Your face," she finished.

"Har-de-har," I said.

Hector stroked his cat's back. "He's been doing that a lot lately."

"What, bringing you roadkill num-nums?" I asked.

Fitz narrowed his eyes. If he wasn't a cat, I would've sworn he was giving me attitude.

"No," said Hector. "His meows have gotten way weird—almost like he's trying to talk."

"Meer *eeer*," said Fitz.

I held up a hand. "Wait. I . . . I think I understand him."

The cat's tail twitched. "*Reoww* rauw rauw."

"What's he saying?" said Hector.

"He's saying 'Kiss . . . my fuzzy . . . fazooski.'"

Hector cracked up.

Steph rolled her eyes. "That's it; I'm going home," she said.

My sister has no sense of humor.

"No," said Hector, "he's saying, 'Foolish humans, bring me mouse pizza!'"

We followed Steph down the sidewalk. Fitz left his lizard and tagged along.

Three doors down from our house, we passed the new construction site. The building was half-finished. It looked like a kindergartner's art project—all lumpy and lopsided. Sandpiles and equipment surrounded it, and a huge cavelike mouth yawned where a front door should've been.

"Your monster condo creeps me out," said Steph.

"I never said it was a monster condo. Just that it seemed weird."

"You should know weird," she said. "You see it whenever you pass a mirror."

Hector sniffed. "Speaking of weird, you smell that? Like someone had beans for lunch? This place always stinks like that."

"And here I thought that was *you*," I said.

Something—a bird? a bat?—fluttered past the cave-mouth door. *Shoom!* It was sucked inside.

"Whoa!" I blurted. *What the heck?*

"Beware," said Hector in a vampire voice. "Dracula's moving to the 'hood."

"You're both so immature," said Stephanie. She snorted and walked on.

Hector and I tore ourselves away. "It would be kinda cool if it *was* a vampire house," I said.

"Anything to jazz up this neighborhood," said Hector.

By the time we met the zombies, he'd want to take that back. But by then, of course, it'd be too late.

Cat and Mouth

When we tramped into the living room, Caitlyn was curled up in an armchair. As usual, she was gabbing on the phone. "He did *not*," she said. "Really? Oh, double *eew*. I can't imagine what she sees in him. He's all, like, monzo puke-oid, and she's such a total muffin. You know what I mean?"

I had no idea what she meant. Caitlyn was a college student.

The TV blasted some commercial with a really short rapper. The music drowned out his lyrics.

"Hey, that's Beefy D," said Hector. "He's the boom."

"The boom?" said Stephanie.

"Like *the bomb*, but exploded. He's opening a new clothing store—nothing but underwear."

"Cool," I said. "I do love a nice pair of tighty-whities."

"That's more than I needed to know about your undies," said Hector.

We stepped forward for a better look.

Just then, Caitlin clicked off the TV. "Hang on, I gotta, like, crack the whip on the brats," she said into the phone. "Okay, blivets, time to pull your weight around here. Zeke, take out the trash and clean up the family room—and I mean *mondo-clean*. Stephanie, pull a Bonnie Brillo and do the dishes, and, like, sweep up."

She clapped twice. "Move it, munchkins!"

Sheesh.

"So, where was I?" she said into the phone. "Oh, yeah, the party . . ." Caitlyn took her mouth into the family room. We took ourselves into the kitchen.

Steph plowed through the breakfast dishes as Hector and I watched. "Aren't you going to get the trash?" she asked.

"I will," I said. "Later."

She shrugged. "It's your funeral."

"How much longer do you have to put up with Queen Kong?" asked Hector.

"Until Mom and Dad get back from the dig," said Stephanie. She took a carrot from the fridge and cleaned it.

(Really. She even eats this way when our parents aren't home. Sick, huh?)

I grabbed a pack of corn chips and tossed another to Hector. "One more week of dear, sweet cousin Caitlyn," I said.

Flip-flup.

The cat door opened. I looked around, hoping to see our cat Meathead—the doofus ran away a couple of weeks ago. But it was just Fitz.

He strutted into the kitchen carrying a bird, then made weird meows like before. Maybe Fitz had been munching on the bird, I don't know, but it had some serious problems. Its head was creased down the middle, like . . .

Well, like a feathered derrière. (I know my teacher keeps telling me to lay off the potty humor, but it's true.)

"Yuck, what's with Fitz and the dead things?" I said.

"Maybe he thinks we're his kittens," said Steph, crunching her carrot.

"Yeah. Well *this* kitten likes burritos," I said.

Hector smirked. "Aha! That smell was *you*!" He opened the door and chucked the bird outside. The cat left, grumbling to himself.

"So," Hector said, "what's the big deal with your aunt?"

"Great-aunt Zenobia?" I said. "Come on."

I led Hector from the kitchen.

"You better not be going into Dad's office," Steph called after us.

We went down the hall and into Dad's office.

"It's like she's psychic or something," said Hector.

"Psycho, maybe," I said.

The room was half museum, half office-supply store, and looked like it had been organized by a cyclone. Blue binders, paper, and Post-its mixed with site maps, fossils, dinosaur toys, an old apple core, and some even older skulls. Archeology books lay everywhere.

I rooted through the layers on the desk. "It was in this stack . . ."

Hector pointed at a kooky antique toilet. Its

carved, fancy bowl held rolled-up maps. It looked like the john of some totally mental medieval king.

"Is this in case the other one breaks down?" he asked.

"Nah, that's just something from Great-aunt— *Aha!*" I pulled an envelope from the mound. Inside was a photo of an old woman in a pith helmet and leather jacket. She sat on a motorcycle, holding a machete. She looked like one tough granny.

"Who is she, Indiana Jones's mother?" said Hector.

"*Was,*" I said. "She died or disappeared or something. I never met her. But her lawyer sent us some of her old stuff." I nodded at the toilet.

"The lawyer sent you her potty? Maybe you're the *butt* of a cruel joke."

I groaned. "Pretty cheeky," I said. "But that's not all of it."

"What's in the letter?" asked Hector.

"The key," I said, "to an A on my family history report."

I led the way back to the living room, and we plopped down on the couch.

"Nice sculpture," said Hector, looking at a jar of rotten bananas on the table.

"That, young Igor, is my science project. I'm making methane gas."

"Just have another burrito," he said. "And since when did you become Dr. Science Nerd?"

"Since my grades laid an egg," I said. I slid the letter from its envelope. "Anyway, check it out: 'We have discovered the most extraordinary artifacts, and—'"

Steph appeared in the doorway.

"That better not be what I think it is," she said.

"Chill, Stephapotamus. I'm just reading to Hector."

"That's for *my* project!" she shrilled. Her fists clenched.

"'The Devil's Punchbowl has proven to be a—,'" I read aloud.

Fitz scampered into the room. "Reeeow!"

Back again? What was up with *him*?

"Give me that!" Steph cried.

"Finders keepers, losers get the blues-ers," I sang, slipping the letter back into its envelope.

The cat leaped onto the coffee table. "*Meer! Mrow, rauw, row!*" He head-butted my banana jar. Once, twice . . .

"No!"

With the third hit, it tumbled off the table and shattered on the tile floor—*kzzshh!*

The stink of methane made my eyes water.

"I'm gonna skin that cat!" I cried.

Just then, the doorbell rang.

And like a dope, I answered it.

Stranger Danger

Two odd men stood on the doorstep. One was tall; one was chubby. They wore identical black suits and dark sunglasses.

That wasn't so weird. But they also wore really cheap fake noses and mustaches—the kind from a bad Halloween costume.

That was weird.

"Greetings," said the tall one. A hairy mole stuck out of his cheek. It was as thick as a thumb.

"We'd like to have a chat with your family," said the other. His gut pushed against his suit buttons.

Steph joined me. "We're not supposed to talk to strangers," she said.

"We're not strangers," said Jelly Belly. "We're government employees."

"You mean *spies*?" said Hector.

"Agents," said Hairy Mole.

The men reached into their coat pockets and took out black leather wallets. Together, they flashed silver badges.

"Wow," I said. "Do you guys practice that, Agent . . . ?"

"No names," said Agent Mole.

"Mrrow, reeuw?" called Fitz from behind us.

"I haven't forgotten about you, cat," I said.

Stephanie frowned at the agents.

Agent Belly tried a smile. "Are your parents home?" he asked.

"No," I said.

"Yes," Steph blurted. We looked at each other.

"And they just finished their, uh, kung fu class. They're both really, really, really high-level . . . um, purple belts."

"Black belts," I said simultaneously.

We traded another quick glance. "Actually, they're more maroon," I said.

Agent Belly smiled again. "Don't worry," he said. "We're talking to everyone on your block. We can stay outside if you prefer."

"We do," I said. Nervously, I tapped Great-aunt Zenobia's letter against my leg.

Agent Mole pulled a notebook and pen from his coat. "Any strangeness?"

"Huh?" I said.

"All the time," said Hector. "Especially when I eat cabbage with—"

"He means," said Agent Belly, "have you noticed anything odd in this neighborhood lately?"

"Like what?" asked Steph.

"Unusual events," said Agent Mole.

"Unusual people," said Agent Belly.

I looked up at him. "Like spies in fake noses at our door?"

The men in black exchanged a look.

"Ha, ha," said Agent Belly.

Fitz bumped against the back of my knees.

"Well, our clocks were off this morning," said Steph.

Mole scribbled in his notebook. "Clocks."

"Meer eeeow," said Fitz.

I glanced behind us. The cat was pacing up and down, *mrow*ing to himself and shaking his head.

"Hey, that's another thing," said Hector. "My cat's been talking up a storm."

"Talking cats," said Agent Mole. "And what does it say?"

Hector shrugged. "Meow?"

"Yeah," I said. "And he's been bringing us road-kill, like—"

Something brushed my hand. Fitz had snatched Great-aunt Zenobia's letter!

He slipped between the agents, then shot down the steps and across the yard. The envelope fluttered in his jaws like a flag.

I took off after him. "Give me that!"

Behind me, Steph said, "Uh, excuse us."

The door slammed. She and Hector trotted after me.

"Fitz!" I called.

We rounded the hedge. The cat was just up the street, sitting calmly.

"Don't spook him," said Steph. We slowed to a brisk walk.

The gap closed. Now we were only ten feet away.

Fitz watched us with wide golden eyes.

Five feet away.

"Nice kitty," I said. "That's it . . ."

I lunged.

Zip! Fitz shot across the street, still carrying the letter.

"Stupid hairball!"

"I'm hurt," said Hector. "He *never* plays fetch with *me.*"

We pounded after the cat.

"Hey, Zeke," said Hector. "I think those guys are after us."

I looked back. Agents Mole and Belly jogged across the street, fake noses askew.

"Kids!" panted Jelly Belly. "Come back here!"

"Yup," I said. "They're after us. Come on!"

Fitz took a sharp left and re-crossed the street.

"Oh no!" said Steph. "He's going into the construction site."

"Stop that cat!" I cried.

But before we could reach him, Fitz slipped through a gap in the fence.

"This is crazy," I muttered. "No cat is *this* mental."

"Wait right there!" cried Agent Belly from across the street.

Oh, *great.* I rattled the gate. It wasn't locked.

"You can't go in there," said Steph. "It's trespassing."

"Would you rather hang out with *them*?" I nodded at the spies.

"I'm coming," she said. "But I'm still right."

The three of us edged into the construction site. We threaded through stacks of lumber, idle cranes, and earthmovers. No Fitz.

"Here, kitty, kitty," said Steph.

"Here, Fitzie, Fitzie," said Hector.

"Here, you furry meatloaf," I said, rounding a pile of sand.

Behind us, the gate clanged. The two agents must have pushed through.

"There!" hissed Steph.

Fitz sat at the front door. The envelope twitched in his mouth.

We closed in.

"Cornered at last," I whispered.

"*There* you are!" came a voice behind us. The two agents stood at either side of the sandpile, fists on hips.

Yeesh!

Fitz retreated through the open door. We followed.

The ripe, beany smell sharpened. A strong wind blew into the building, plucking at my clothes.

The plywood floor creaked and shifted under our feet.

"Don't go in there!" called Agent Belly. "It's not safe!"

Hector jumped forward and grabbed Fitz. "Gotcha!"

As he hit the floor, it tilted like a slide at a water park. A cement basin lay beneath the plywood. A dark opening gaped in the center.

Steph and I went slipping down toward Hector and Fitz.

"Hey," I tried to say, but it came out "Aiyeeeee!"

And we tumbled—neighbor, cat, sister, and all—down into a black, black hole.

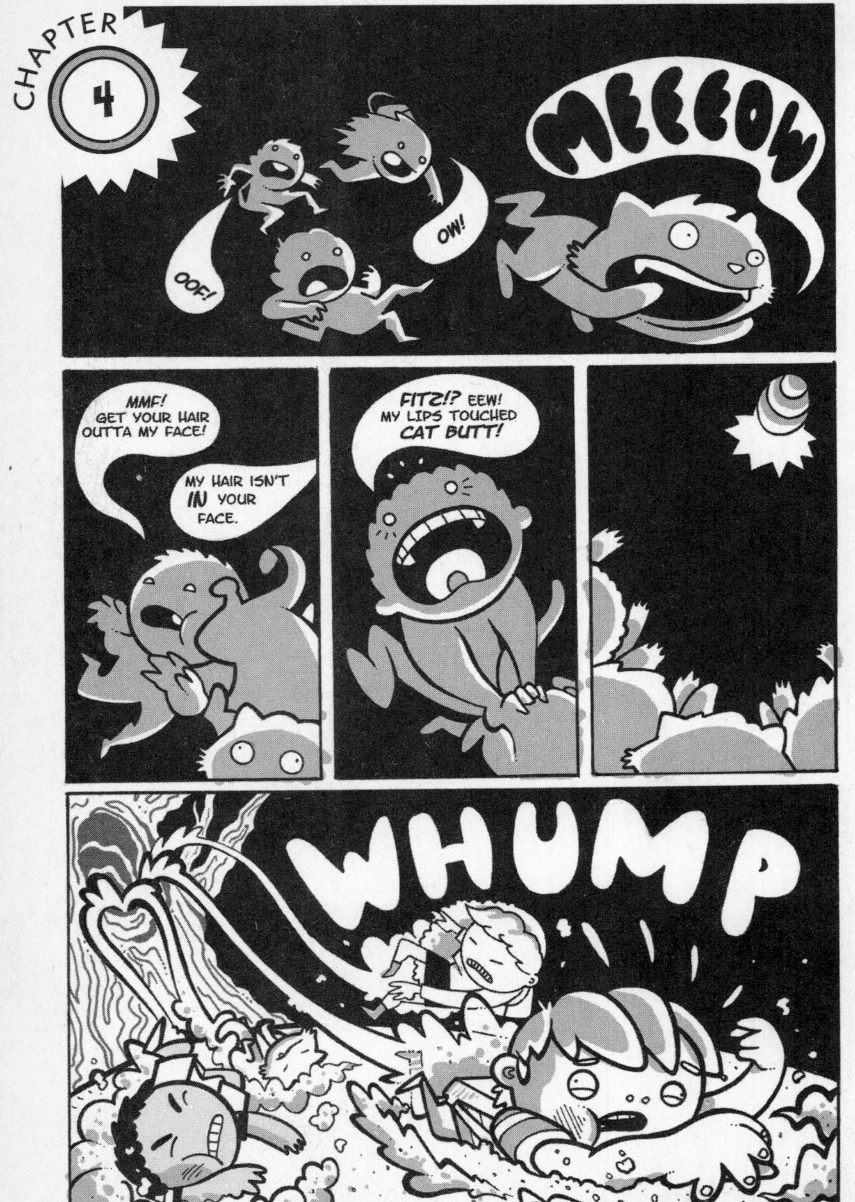
CHAPTER 4
OOF!
OW!
MEEEOW
MMF! GET YOUR HAIR OUTTA MY FACE!
MY HAIR ISN'T IN YOUR FACE.
FITZ!? EEW! MY LIPS TOUCHED CAT BUTT!
WHUMP

EEUGH! MY BUTT TOUCHED HUMAN LIPS.

WHO SAID THAT?

FITZ?

FITZ?! SINCE WHEN CAN YOU *TALK?*

I MUST BATHE IMMEDIATELY.

HMPH. NOTHING GETS BY YOU.

UH, GUYS? WE'VE GOT WORSE PROBLEMS THAN A TALKING CAT.

WHAT DO YOU MEAN?

LOOK!

WHA--?

WHERE IN THE WORLD ARE WE?

EXACTLY. YOU'RE *IN* THE WORLD.

IMPOSSIBLE...

OOH, LISTEN TO LITTLE MISS EXPERT.

BUT THERE'S, UH, MOLTEN LAVA AND UM... *DIRT* INSIDE THE EARTH.

LOTS OF DIRT.

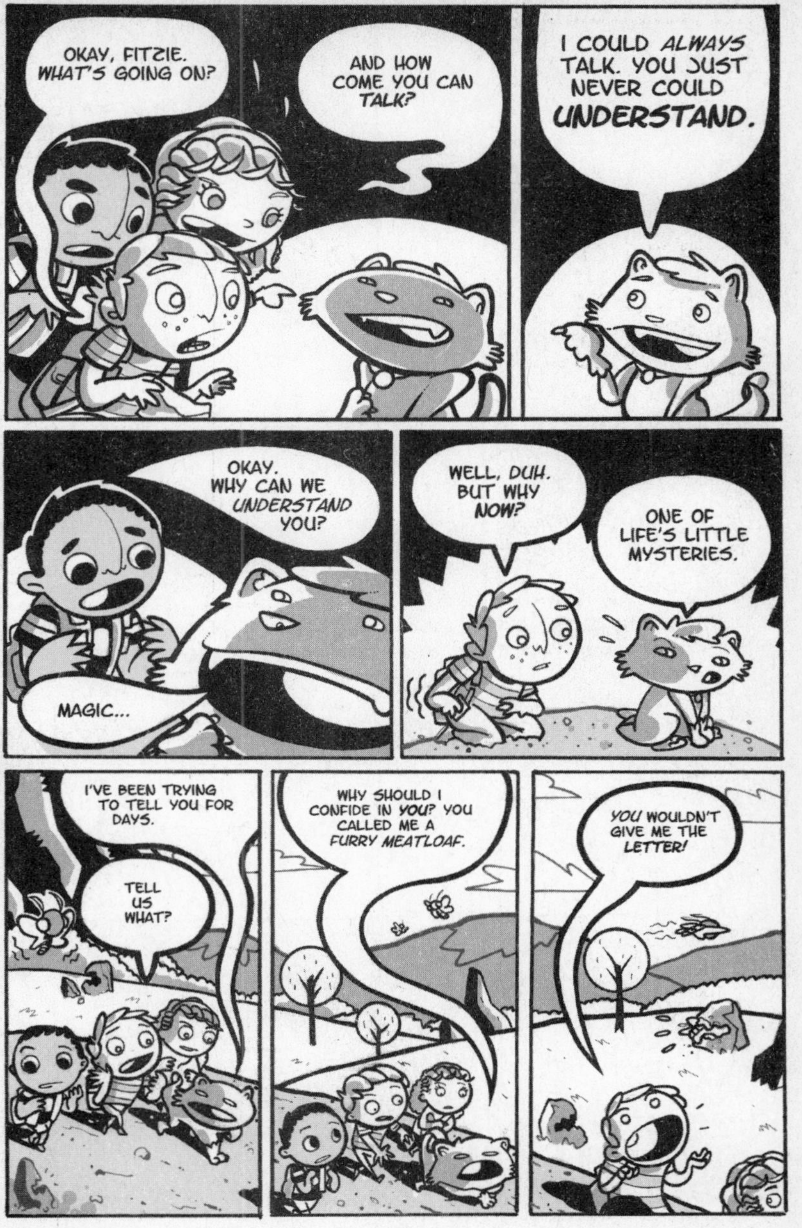

OKAY, FITZIE. WHAT'S GOING ON?
AND HOW COME YOU CAN TALK?
I COULD ALWAYS TALK. YOU JUST NEVER COULD UNDERSTAND.
OKAY. WHY CAN WE UNDERSTAND YOU?
MAGIC...
WELL, DUH. BUT WHY NOW?
ONE OF LIFE'S LITTLE MYSTERIES.
I'VE BEEN TRYING TO TELL YOU FOR DAYS.
TELL US WHAT?
WHY SHOULD I CONFIDE IN YOU? YOU CALLED ME A FURRY MEATLOAF.
YOU WOULDN'T GIVE ME THE LETTER!

A POWERFUL MAGICAL OBJECT HAS BEEN MUTATING OUR NEIGHBOURHOOD.

OH, REALLY? HOW ABOUT THE DEFORMED BIRDS AND LIZARDS? THE TROUBLE WITH YOUR CLOCKS?

WHAT?! NO WAY WOULD WE HAVE MISSED THAT.

OH.

SO THAT'S WHY THOSE AGENTS SHOWED UP.

I TRIED TO WARN YOU THEY WERE-- OOH, THAT'S NICE--UP TO NO GOOD.

BUT WHY OUR NEIGHBORHOOD?

YEAH, AND WHAT'S THE MAGICAL DOODAD?

PRRRR... I HAVEN'T THE VAGUEST--DON'T STOP--IDEA.

SO, WHERE THE HECK ARE WE?

I SUGGEST YOU ASK... THEM.

THEM?

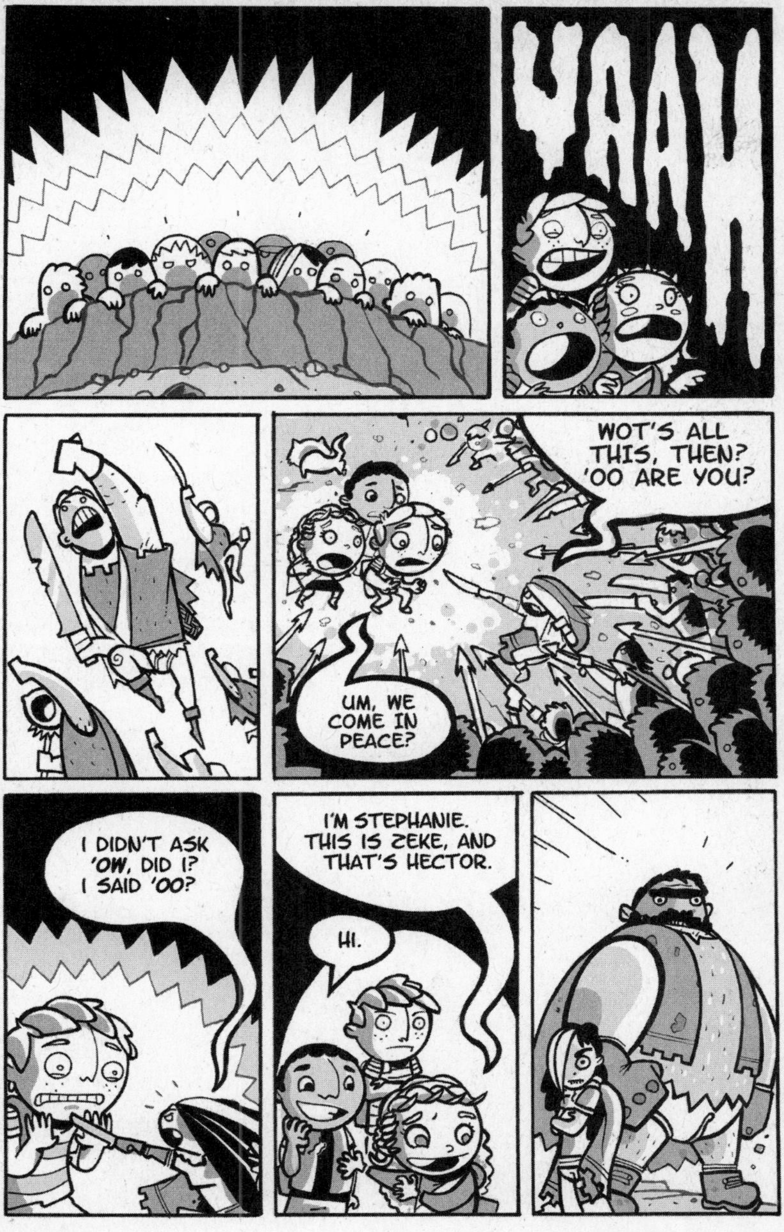
YAAY
WOT'S ALL THIS, THEN? 'OO ARE YOU?
UM, WE COME IN PEACE?
I DIDN'T ASK *'OW*, DID I? I SAID *'OO*?
I'M STEPHANIE. THIS IS ZEKE, AND THAT'S HECTOR.
HI.

WHERE'S YOUR UNDIES?

UM, WHERE DO YOU THINK? UNDER OUR CLOTHES.

THAT'S LOONY. NOBODY WEARS 'EM UNDERNEATH.

THEY DO WHERE WE COME FROM— ON EARTH.

YOU KNOW, UP ABOVE?

UP ABOVE?

THEY'RE LYIN', ALF.

I'D SAY LYIN', WHITEY.

WE'RE NOT LYING!

WOT SAY WE GIVE 'EM ALL WEDGIES TILL THEY CONFESS?

YEAH! THAT'S THE BLOOMIN' WAY! WEDGIES!

CAN'T YOU JUST TAKE OUR WORD FOR IT?

WE'RE REBELS.

WE'RE AT WAR. AND YOU COULD BE WORKIN' FOR 'IM.

IM? WHO'S IM?

NOT IM, 'IM!

THE **UNDERLORD**, AS IF YOU DIDN'T KNOW. THE EVIL WIZARD WOT'S TURNIN' UNDIES INTO ZOMBIES!

HOW IS THAT EVEN POSSIBLE?

ENOUGH BLABBER. IT'S **WEDGIE TIME!**

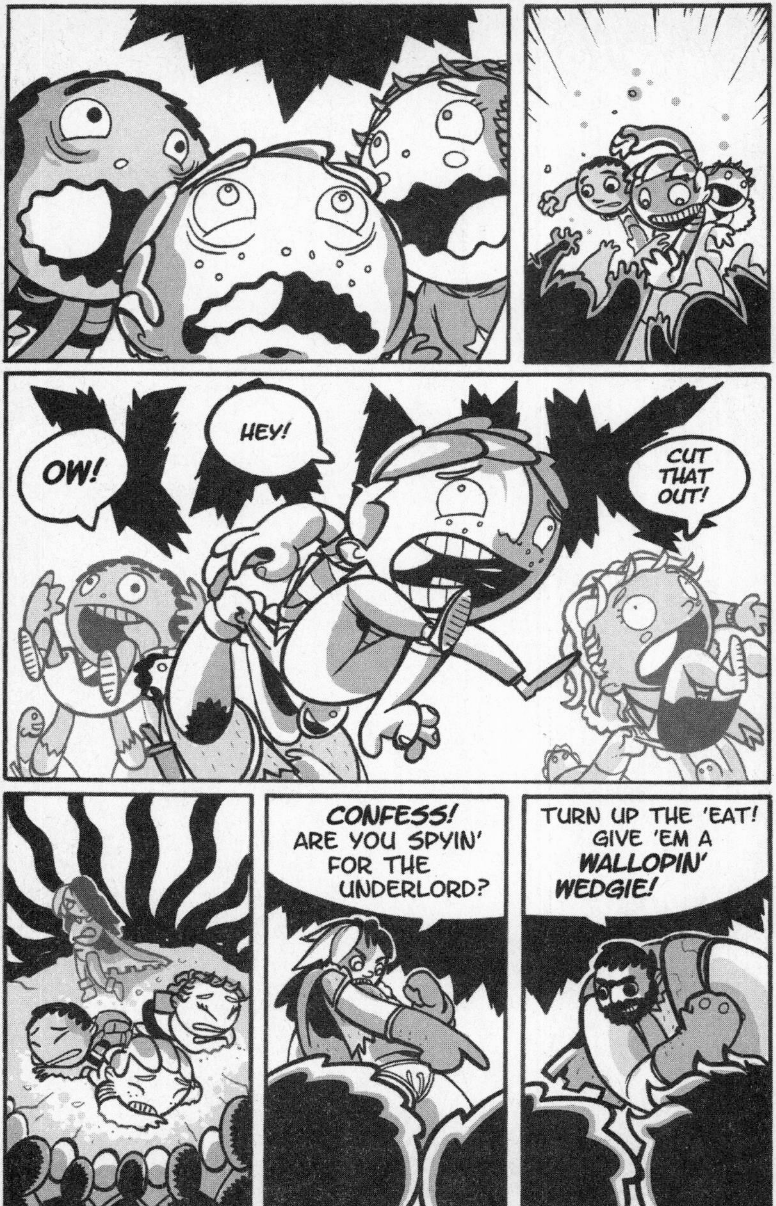

OW!
HEY!
CUT THAT OUT!
CONFESS! ARE YOU SPYIN' FOR THE UNDERLORD?
TURN UP THE 'EAT! GIVE 'EM A WALLOPIN' WEDGIE!

WAIT!

WOT?

THE MARK!

THE PROPHECY...

WHAT?

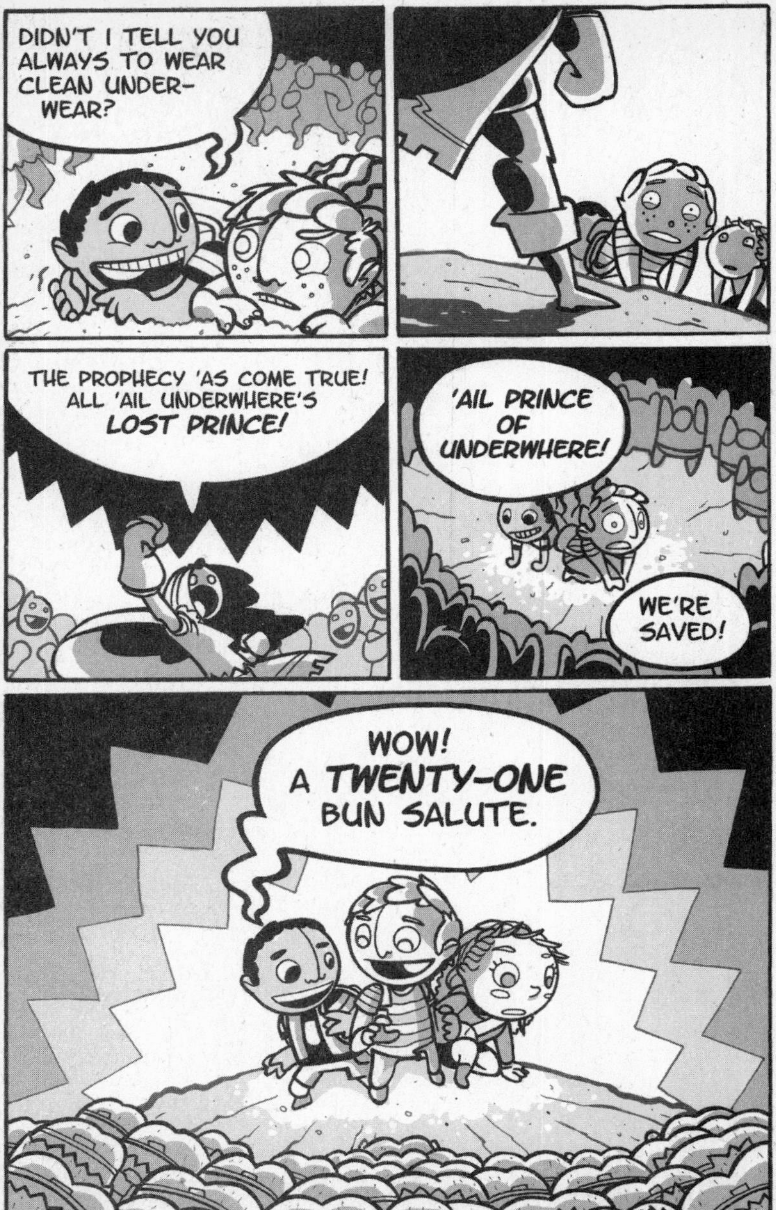
DIDN'T I TELL YOU ALWAYS TO WEAR CLEAN UNDER-WEAR?
THE PROPHECY 'AS COME TRUE! ALL 'AIL UNDERWHERE'S LOST PRINCE!
'AIL PRINCE OF UNDERWHERE!
WE'RE SAVED!
WOW! A TWENTY-ONE BUN SALUTE.

IT'S JUST AS *THE BOOK OF BOOTY* FORETOLD!

"AND IN THE DARK DAYS, THE LOST PRINCE OF UNDER-WHERE SHALL RETURN."

"AND YE SHALL KNOW 'IM BY THE FRUIT ON 'IS GARMENTS."

FRUIT OF THE *LOOM?*

"AND 'E SHALL BE FROM ANOTHER PLACE AND NOT KNOW YOU."

THAT'S YOU, PRINCE... UMM, WOT'S YOUR NAME AGAIN?

'E'S COME TO FREE US FROM THE UNDER-LORD'S RULE!

ZEKE.

ALL 'AIL PRINCE ZEKE!!!

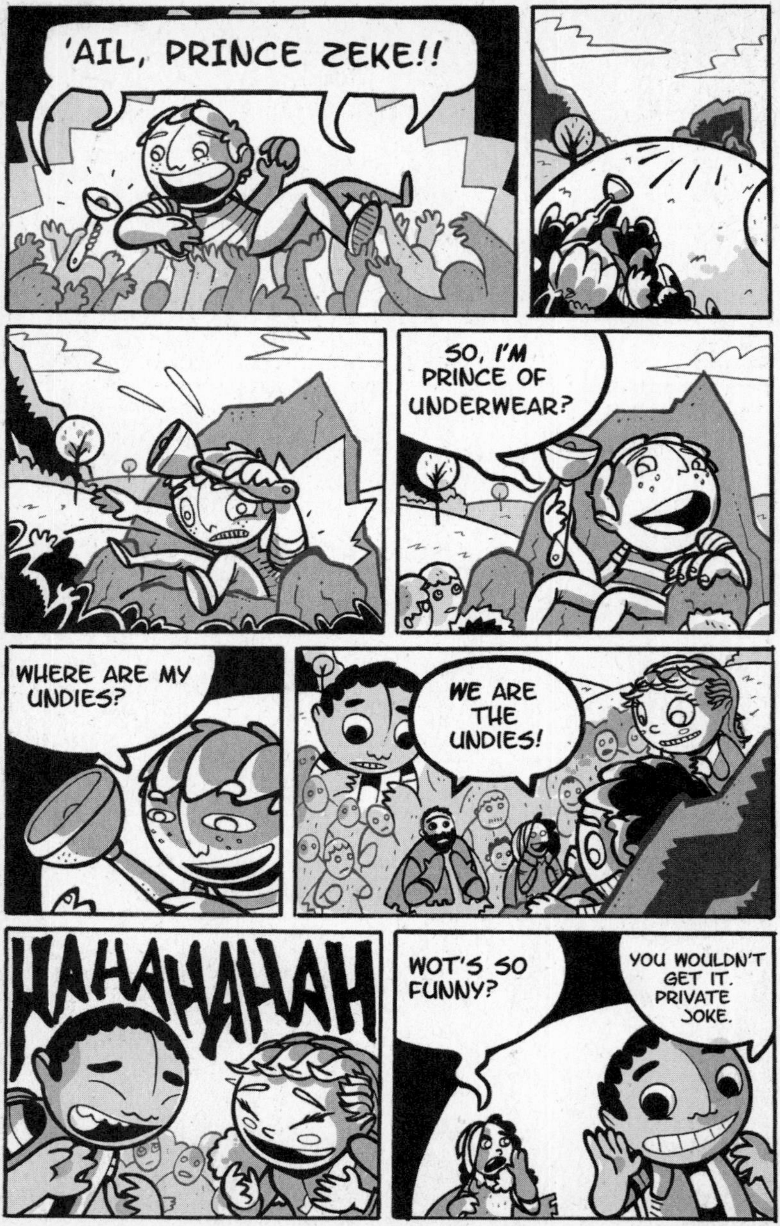
'AIL, PRINCE ZEKE!!
SO, I'M PRINCE OF UNDERWEAR?
WHERE ARE MY UNDIES?
WE ARE THE UNDIES!
HAHAHAHAH
WOT'S SO FUNNY?
YOU WOULDN'T GET IT. PRIVATE JOKE.

WHY ARE YOU CALLED UNDIES?

FOR OUR CLOTHIN'—IT'S SO FAMOUS EVEN UPLANDERS WEAR IT.

AND FOR UNDERWHERE. THIS PLACE.

SO IF HE'S THE LOST PRINCE OF UNDERWHERE, I MUST BE THE LOST PRINCESS.

EH? 'OO ARE YOU?

ZEKE'S SISTER.

PROPHECY DIDN'T SAY NOTHIN' ABOUT NO PRINCESS.

DOESN'T MATTER. A PRINCE'S SISTER IS A PRINCESS.

'COURSE YOU'RE A LOST PRINCESS, LUV.

HEY, WHAT ABOUT ME? DON'T I GET TO BE A LOST SOMETHING?

YOU MEAN, LIKE THE LOST CAT OWNER?

NO, MORE LIKE... THE LOST DIDGERIDOO PLAYER.

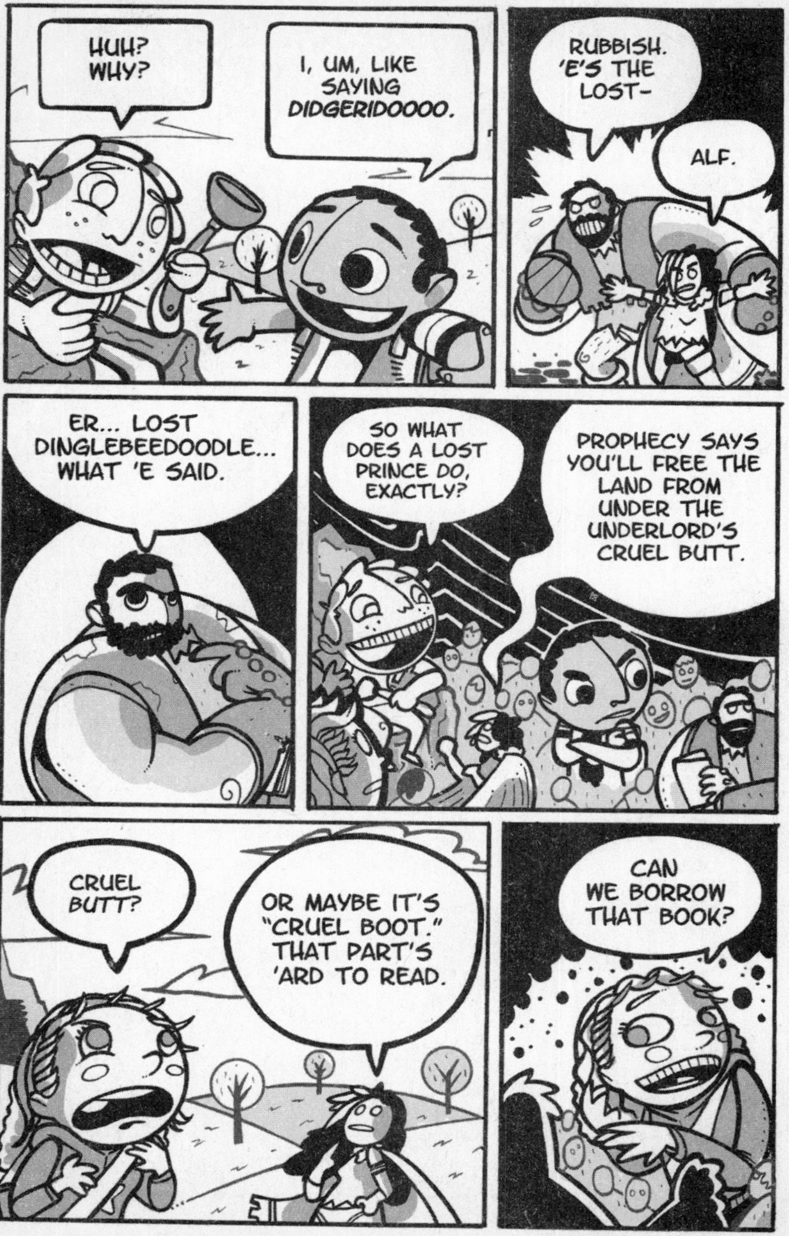
HUH? WHY?
I, UM, LIKE SAYING DIDGERIDOOOO.
RUBBISH. 'E'S THE LOST-
ALF.
ER... LOST DINGLEBEEDOODLE... WHAT 'E SAID.
SO WHAT DOES A LOST PRINCE DO, EXACTLY?
PROPHECY SAYS YOU'LL FREE THE LAND FROM UNDER THE UNDERLORD'S CRUEL BUTT.
CRUEL BUTT?
OR MAYBE IT'S "CRUEL BOOT." THAT PART'S 'ARD TO READ.
CAN WE BORROW THAT BOOK?

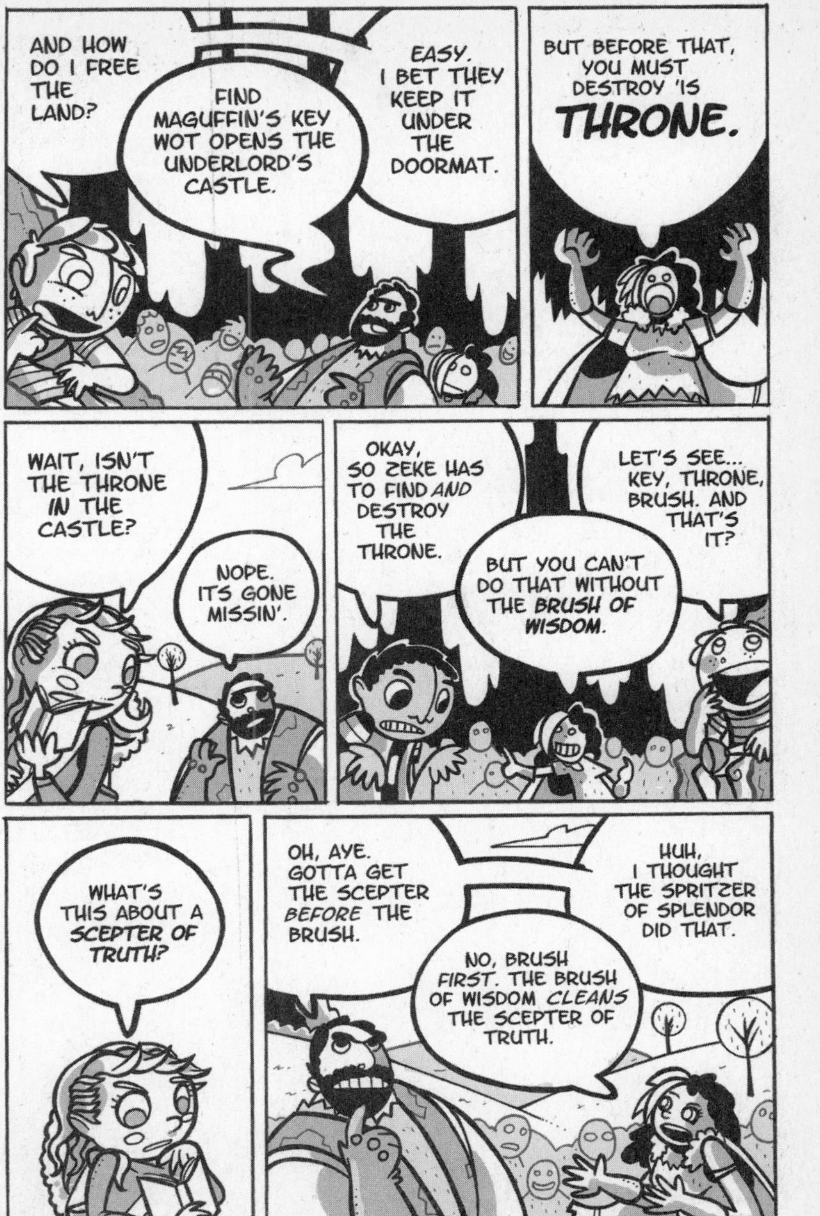
AND HOW DO I FREE THE LAND?
FIND MAGUFFIN'S KEY WOT OPENS THE UNDERLORD'S CASTLE.
EASY. I BET THEY KEEP IT UNDER THE DOORMAT.
BUT BEFORE THAT, YOU MUST DESTROY 'IS THRONE.
WAIT, ISN'T THE THRONE IN THE CASTLE?
NOPE. IT'S GONE MISSIN'.
OKAY, SO ZEKE HAS TO FIND AND DESTROY THE THRONE.
BUT YOU CAN'T DO THAT WITHOUT THE BRUSH OF WISDOM.
LET'S SEE... KEY, THRONE, BRUSH. AND THAT'S IT?
WHAT'S THIS ABOUT A SCEPTER OF TRUTH?
OH, AYE. GOTTA GET THE SCEPTER BEFORE THE BRUSH.
NO, BRUSH FIRST. THE BRUSH OF WISDOM CLEANS THE SCEPTER OF TRUTH.
HUH, I THOUGHT THE SPRITZER OF SPLENDOR DID THAT.

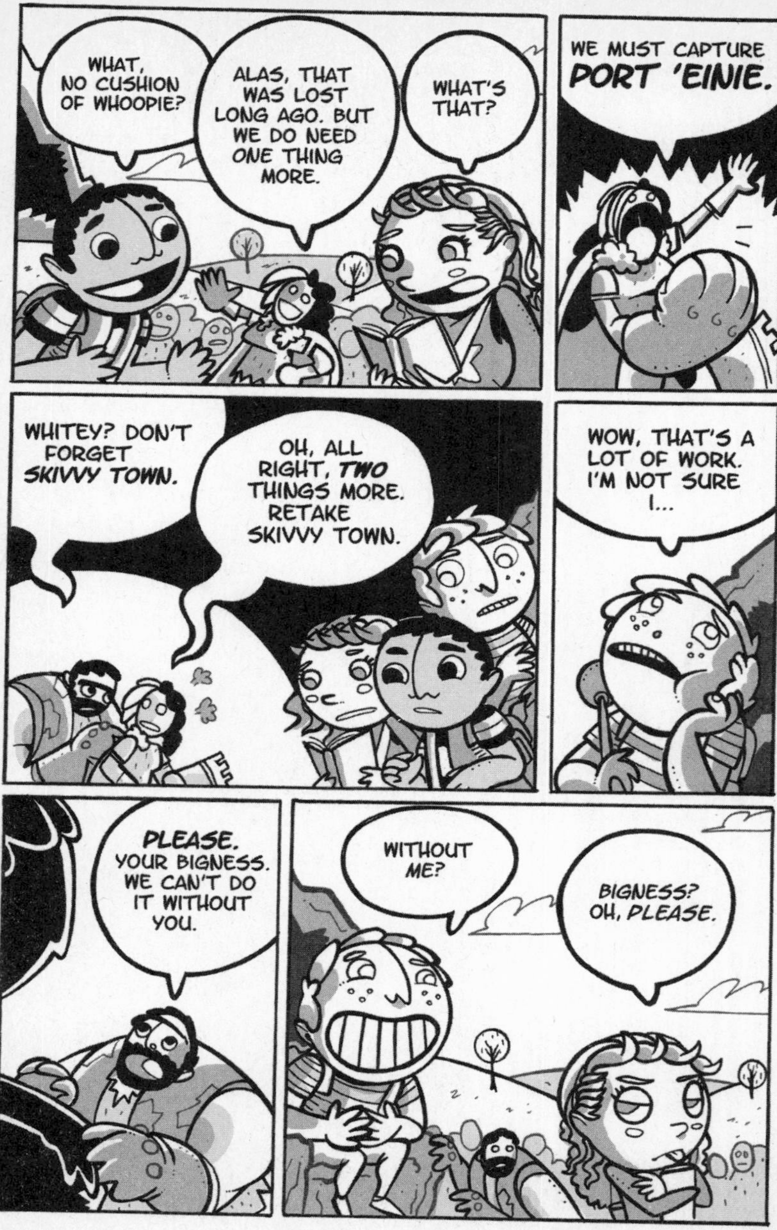
WHAT, NO CUSHION OF WHOOPIE?
ALAS, THAT WAS LOST LONG AGO. BUT WE DO NEED ONE THING MORE.
WHAT'S THAT?
WE MUST CAPTURE PORT 'EINIE.
WHITEY? DON'T FORGET SKIVVY TOWN.
OH, ALL RIGHT, TWO THINGS MORE. RETAKE SKIVVY TOWN.
WOW, THAT'S A LOT OF WORK. I'M NOT SURE I...
PLEASE. YOUR BIGNESS. WE CAN'T DO IT WITHOUT YOU.
WITHOUT ME?
BIGNESS? OH, PLEASE.

SO SKIVVY TOWN IS A *CASTLE?*

ONE OF THE BLOOMIN' BIGGEST!

COOL! I'LL HELP YOU STORM THE CASTLE.

DO YOU PROMISE?

SURE.

DO YOU GIVE US YOUR MOST SACRED OATH?

WHY NOT?

DO YOU SWEAR BY ALL WOT'S PRINCELY AND...NOBLE-ISH AND...COTTONY FRESH?

ALL RIGHT, ALREADY, I *SWEAR.* HOW HARD CAN IT BE?

THE CASTLE IS FULL OF ZOMBIES AND THE UNDERLORD'S SOLDIERS.

OH, NO.

OH YES. AND WE'LL 'AVE TO WATCH OUT FOR.....*THE THUNDER LIZARDS!*

OOH, THUNDER LIZARDS!

NASTY BEASTS!

DON'T LIKE 'EM!

WHAT'S A THUNDER LIZARD?

ROOOOOAR

THUNDER LIZARDS!

AAAH!

RUN!

MEET US RIGHT 'ERE, THIS TIME TOMORROW! NOW *GO!*

BAAARGH

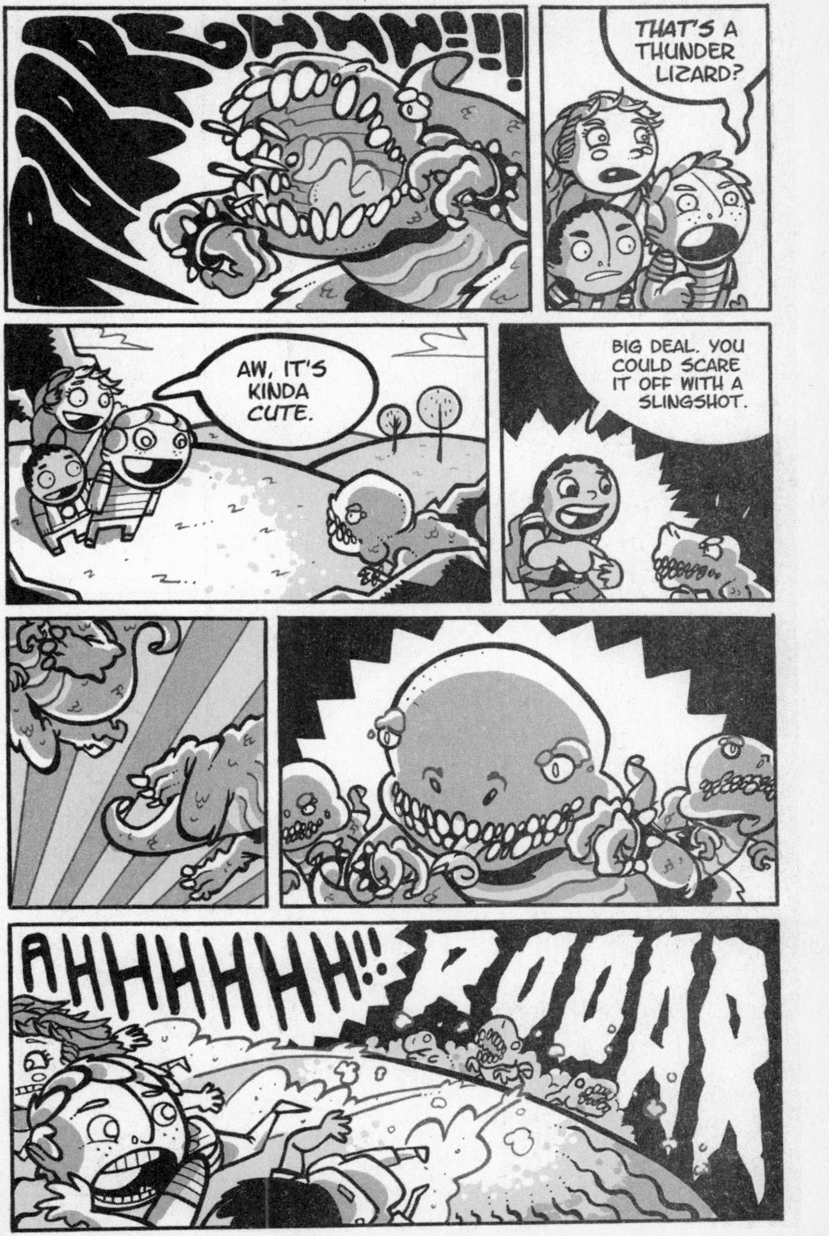
RAAGHHH!!!
THAT'S A THUNDER LIZARD?
AW, IT'S KINDA CUTE.
BIG DEAL. YOU COULD SCARE IT OFF WITH A SLINGSHOT.
AHHHHHH!!
ROOAR

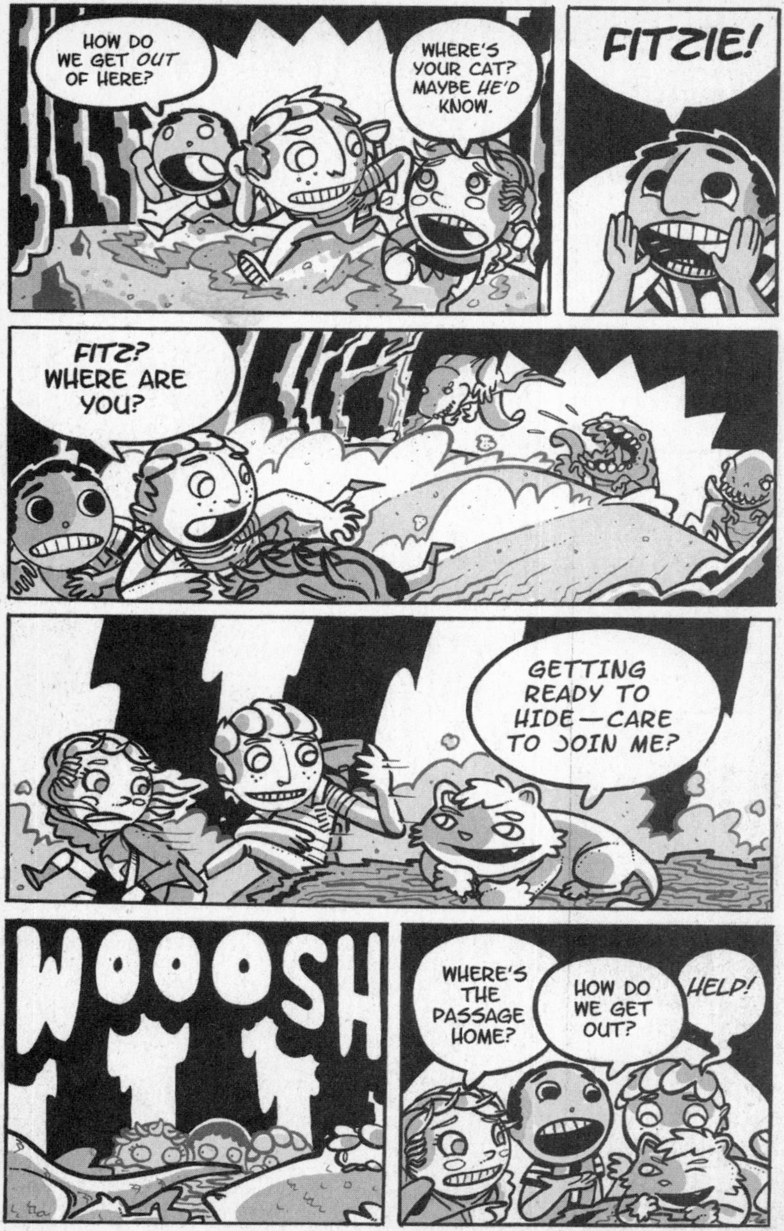

HOW DO WE GET OUT OF HERE?
WHERE'S YOUR CAT? MAYBE HE'D KNOW.
FITZIE!
FITZ? WHERE ARE YOU?
GETTING READY TO HIDE—CARE TO JOIN ME?
WOOOSH
WHERE'S THE PASSAGE HOME?
HOW DO WE GET OUT?
HELP!

I *SUPPOSE* WE COULD GO. IT IS NEARLY *SUPPER TIME*, AFTER ALL.

ANYTHING YOU WANT! JUST GET US HOME.

MMM. I'VE ALWAYS FANCIED *CAVIAR*.

YOU GOT IT! WITH A CHERRY ON TOP!

HURRY!

ROARGHH

THEY'RE COMING BACK!

THIS PLACE SUCKS.

YOU GOT THAT RIGHT.

NO, MOUSE-BRAIN. *SUCTION-MAGICAL* ENERGY. IT MIGHT TAKE US BACK.

MIGHT?! YOU DON'T KNOW?

IM A CAT. NOT A SCIENTIST.

THEY'VE SPOTTED US!

HERE GOES NOTHING.

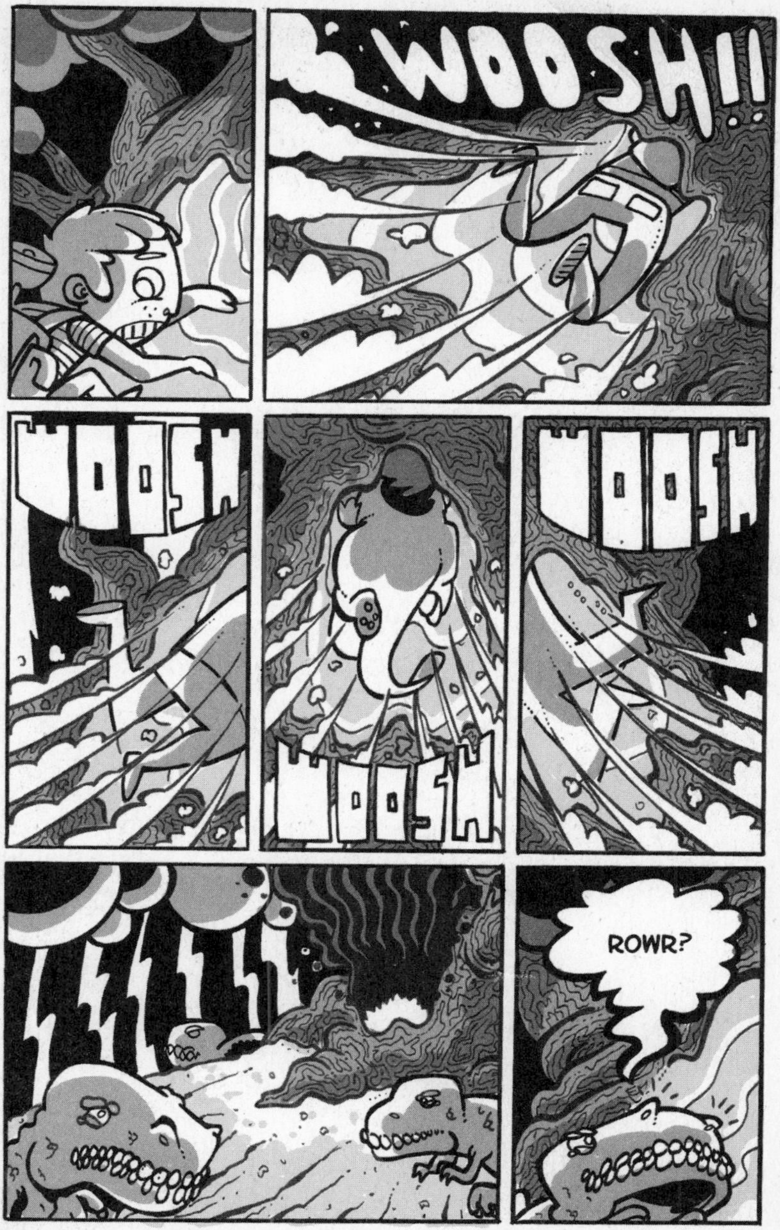
WOOSH!!
WOOSH
WOOSH
WOOSH
ROWR?

I Spy Trouble

Ptoo! Ptoo! Ptoo! Ptoo!

The tube spat us out in a hurry. We shot from a hole in the floor and landed in a heap on the plywood deck.

"That . . . ," gasped Steph.

"Was close," I said. (One of the few times we've ever completed each other's sentences.)

Hector gave a shaky grin. "I'll never feel the same way about Barney again."

We stumbled from the construction site, through the fence, and out to the street. Fitz followed.

But when we reached the curb, we noticed something: It wasn't our street!

"Where are we?" I said.

Hector looked down at Fitz. "Well?" he asked. "Any ideas?"

"Meer mrow," said Fitz.

I wagged a finger. "Don't play kittycat with me," I said. "Speak!"

Fitz rolled his eyes. "Mrowwww," he drawled.

"He *is* speaking," said Steph. "But we can only understand him down *there*."

The cat gave us a *well, duh* expression.

"I knew that," I said.

Steph headed for a street sign at the corner. "Cherry and Wilkins," she said.

Hector scratched his head. "We're on the other side of the school. How did *that* happen?"

Nobody had an answer.

We began the long walk home. I was so

distracted, I barely noticed the figures in the black stretch Humvee.

But as we later found out, they sure noticed us.

Twenty minutes later, we reached our street: good ol' Vista View Lane.

"What now?" Hector said.

"We tell someone," said Steph. "Caitlyn."

I shook my head. "No way."

"Zeke—"

"She'll say we can't go down there anymore. Or she'll blab to some TV station and hog all the glory."

I'd never had anything this special happen to me. And I for sure didn't want to share it with Queen Kong. No way, nohow.

Steph chewed her lip. At last, she said, "*Maybe* you've got a point, but—"

"Well, well," said a deep voice. "You're back."

We turned. Agent Jelly Belly stood on the sidewalk.

"Time for that little chat," he said.

"Sorry," I said, "gotta run. Tons of homework."

The chubby spy smiled. "I wouldn't go anywhere just yet."

Agent Mole stepped into view. Trapped in his arms was Fitz.

"*Mwrrr,*" the cat moaned through a muzzle. He was not a happy kitty.

"Fitzie!" Hector cried. He stepped forward.

Agent Belly held up a finger. "Ah-ah-ah," he said. "First we get some answers, then you get the cat."

Fitz struggled, but Mole held tight.

"Okay," I said. "Ask your questions."

Belly frowned and adjusted his fake nose. "You disappeared down that hole. Then you returned from another direction. Where did you go?"

Hector looked back at Steph and me. His eyes begged.

Steph gave a little nod.

"Underwhere," said Hector.

I let out the breath I'd been holding.

"Didn't ask what you're wearing," said Agent Mole.

"Not underwear, *Underwhere*," said Hector.

"It's a land down below," said Stephanie.

The two agents exchanged a look.

"Interesting," said Mole. "Continue."

Between us, we told them the whole story.

Belly and Mole almost smiled. They whispered together with their backs to us. Then they turned.

"Listen up, kids," said Agent Belly. "You're going back to your . . . Underwhere-land and gathering information for us."

Steph put her hands on her hips. "What do we get out of it?"

"Your cat," said Agent Mole, squeezing Fitz.

"*Mwwrrr.*"

"And the warm fuzzy feeling of helping your country," added Belly.

"Why don't *you* go down there yourselves?" asked Hector.

"We tried," said Mole. "We can't."

Agent Belly shrugged. "The hole won't let us. One of life's little mysteries."

"That's not our problem," I said. "Why don't you find someone else to spy for you?"

Belly looked from Steph to me. "Your parents rely on government grants for their work. It would be such a shame if those grants . . . dried up."

"You wouldn't dare," said Stephanie.

"Wouldn't we?"

Yeesh. Now it was our turn to huddle and whisper.

I stepped forward. "We'll do it," I said.

"Just stay away from our parents," said Stephanie.

"Goody," said Agent Mole. He set the cat down and released the muzzle.

Fitz promptly bit the man and ran off.

Agent Belly reached into his jacket. "You'll need some gear," he said, pulling out a silver cylinder. "Camera pen. It downloads to a PC."

I took it.

"Where's mine?" said Hector.

Agent Mole gave him a yellowish-brown blob. "Ear recorder."

"Disgusting," said Steph. "It looks like earwax."

"Pop it into your ear," said Belly. "One poke for *on*; two pokes for *off*."

Hector studied the blob on his palm. "Gee, thanks."

"Hey, what about me?" asked Stephanie.

"Here," said Agent Belly, handing her a shiny

black card with white lettering. It had a name and phone number I couldn't make out. "Report to us every day."

"*Every* day?" I said.

Steph took it. "*HUSH?*" she said.

"Hush, yourself, Stephadorkus."

"No, Midget Boy, H.U.S.H." She showed me the card.

"Oh."

"What's that stand for?" asked Hector.

"It's, um, top secret," said Agent Mole.

"*Hmph,*" I said to Hector. "Bet he doesn't know."

Mole frowned at Belly, who raised a shoulder. Then, the two spies spun and marched down the sidewalk.

"What are we getting into?" Steph murmured.

"Undercover in Underwhere." I grinned. "Anything can happen."

CHAPTER

6

Melvin's Rap

All that night and into the next day, I could hardly contain myself. Finally, I wasn't the lazy twin, the dumb twin, Stephanie's short brother.

I was a lost prince. I had sworn to help my people storm a castle.

Compared to that, schoolwork wasn't exactly thrilling.

"Zeke? Zeke!" said a voice. "I'm waiting for an answer."

"Huh?" I looked up. Mrs. Ricotta stood at the blackboard.

"*Huh* was not the answer I was looking for," she said.

My face burned.

The class laughed. Melvin Prang twisted in his seat and sneered.

"Smooth one, shrimp," he said. "Did you take dumbo pills today?"

School was definitely less fun than Underwhere.

And our teacher's next announcement didn't improve things.

"Remember, class," said Mrs. Ricotta, "science projects are due on Friday. This counts for fifty percent of your grade, so *certain students* better do very well indeed." For some reason, she looked right at me when she said that.

(Okay, I know the reason. My only decent grade is in English, and that's just because of the class play.)

I groaned. Fitz had trashed my methane experiment. I'd have to think of something science-y, and quick.

At late recess, Steph, Hector, and I met outside the lunchroom. Kids streamed past, headed for the playground. The *shush shush* of the custodian's sweeping echoed down the hall.

"This ear recorder is *sweet*," Hector said. "I've already taped Kevin burping, Ashley gossiping about Chantal, and—"

"You're supposed to use it for spy business," said Steph.

"I'm practicing with monkey business," said Hector.

I gritted my teeth. "This isn't funny. We've got to figure out how to take over a castle. I promised the Undies."

"Since when does a promise mean anything to *you*?" said Steph.

"Since . . . I don't know," I said. She had a point. I'm not always Mr. Reliable. But . . . "Since now," I said. "Since I gave my sacred oath."

"Well, *I* didn't," said Stephanie. "Let's spy for a couple days and call it quits."

"You can do *whatever*," I said, "but *we're* helping the Undies free Skivvy Town. Right, Hector?"

He hesitated, looking from me to Steph. "Uh, that's right!" Hector said at last.

Stephanie pulled back her curly hair. "Oh, really?" she said. "And just what do *you* two know about storming castles?"

"Plenty," I said. "We've been playing video games for years."

"Hah." Steph turned away. She'd never appreciated my skills.

Then we noticed the shaggy-haired custodian, Mr. Wheener. He had stopped sweeping and was watching us.

"He's creepy," whispered Stephanie.

I waved to the janitor. "What's up, Mr. Wheener?"

His face clouded. "*Veener*," he snapped. "It's pronounced *Veener*. How many times I tell you kids?!"

"Guess we forgot," said Hector, keeping a straight face.

Mr. Wheener continued sweeping and mumbling.

"Think he overheard us?" asked Steph.

"No," I said. "And if he did, so what?"

"Yeah," said Hector. "It's not like he knows about Underwhere."

After the last bell rang, I left class as fast as I could.

But not fast enough.

"Yo, yo, midget!" Melvin Prang's voice froze me outside the door.

Yeesh. Why couldn't I have been born six feet tall?

I turned to face him. "I'm not a midget," I muttered. Melvin and his buddy Darryl towered over me. "I'm just shorter than average."

"What's the rush?" said Melvin. "An emergency dwarf meeting?"

Darryl chuckled like that was the funniest thing he'd heard. Why do bully sidekicks always do this? Don't they have a real sense of humor?

"I've, uh, gotta get home," I said. I turned away.

Melvin's meaty hand clamped onto my shoulder. "Not so fast, padangle."

My heart thumped unevenly. Past the bullies, Steph and Hector watched.

"Wh-what do you want?" I said. I hated that my voice wobbled.

Melvin's other hand clenched into a fist. "A rap."

"Why hit me?" I said. "I didn't do anything."

The big meathead snorted. "Not a rap, a *rap*. You wrote songs for that dumb class play, so you can write for me. I wanna win Beefy D's bad-evil contest."

"Bad-evil?" I said.

Darryl leaned down into my face. "That awesome *contest*, moron." His breath smelled of salami and sweat socks. I winced. "Whoever writes the best rap gets to be on TV at Beefy D's grand opening. *Duh*."

"It's due Thursday," said Melvin. He squeezed my shoulder extra hard. "I wanna win, shrimp. Or you'll get the other kind of rap."

I didn't care what he wanted. But I did care about my health.

"Uh, I'll try," I mumbled.

Melvin slapped my back, hard. "Now beat it!" he said. "Get to work, yo!"

Yo? What a yo-yo.

I joined my sister and Hector.

"You should stand up to that punk," said Stephanie. She tossed her curls.

"Are you gonna pay his hospital bills when he does?" asked Hector.

I stomped across the grass. "Let's just get out of here."

Ten minutes later, we dumped our schoolbooks at home. I checked the clock. It was almost time to meet the Undies.

I hustled Steph and Hector over to the construction site. Fitz followed, ears up and eyes moving. Probably watching for the spies.

We stopped by the fence. Across the street, a black stretch Humvee waited at the curb.

"Those agents better leave us alone," said Steph. She stepped toward it.

I caught her arm. "That's not their car."

"He's right," said Hector. "And the sooner we get down under, the sooner we can ditch whoever that is."

Steph glared at the Humvee, but she gave in. We pushed through the gate, marched up to the weird structure, and stepped into its wide mouth.

Hector's nose wrinkled. "Why does this place always stink so much?"

"Guess it's just one of life's little mysteries," I said.

Stephanie sighed. "I wish we had a better way to get down there."

"Like what?" I said. "Taking the elevator?"

She shrugged. "It's just so . . ."

"Dirty?" said Hector.

"Undignified," she said. "But if we must . . ."

"We must," I said.

And so we did. One by one, we approached the hole in the corner. Its suction pulled at us; its stench teased; then—*pop pop pop pop*—down into Underwhere we went.

CHAPTER 7

PROBABLY IN HIS DRESSER DRAWER. HA HA!

HAR-DE-HAR. THEY'RE, UH... WHERE ARE THEY, FITZ?

OKAY, PRINCE. WHERE ARE YOUR UNDIES?

DO I LOOK LIKE UNDERWHERE 411? I DON'T EVEN LIKE THIS PLACE.

THEN WHY'D YOU COME ALONG?

FOR THE PLEASURE OF TELLING YOU ALL HOW VERY STUPID YOU ARE.

UM, I THINK THE ROCKY AREA IS THIS WAY.

LEAD ON, PRINCE FRUIT OF THE LOOM.

ANYBODY?

HELLO

HEAR THAT? FOOTSTEPS.

TROOMP!!!

TROOMP!!!

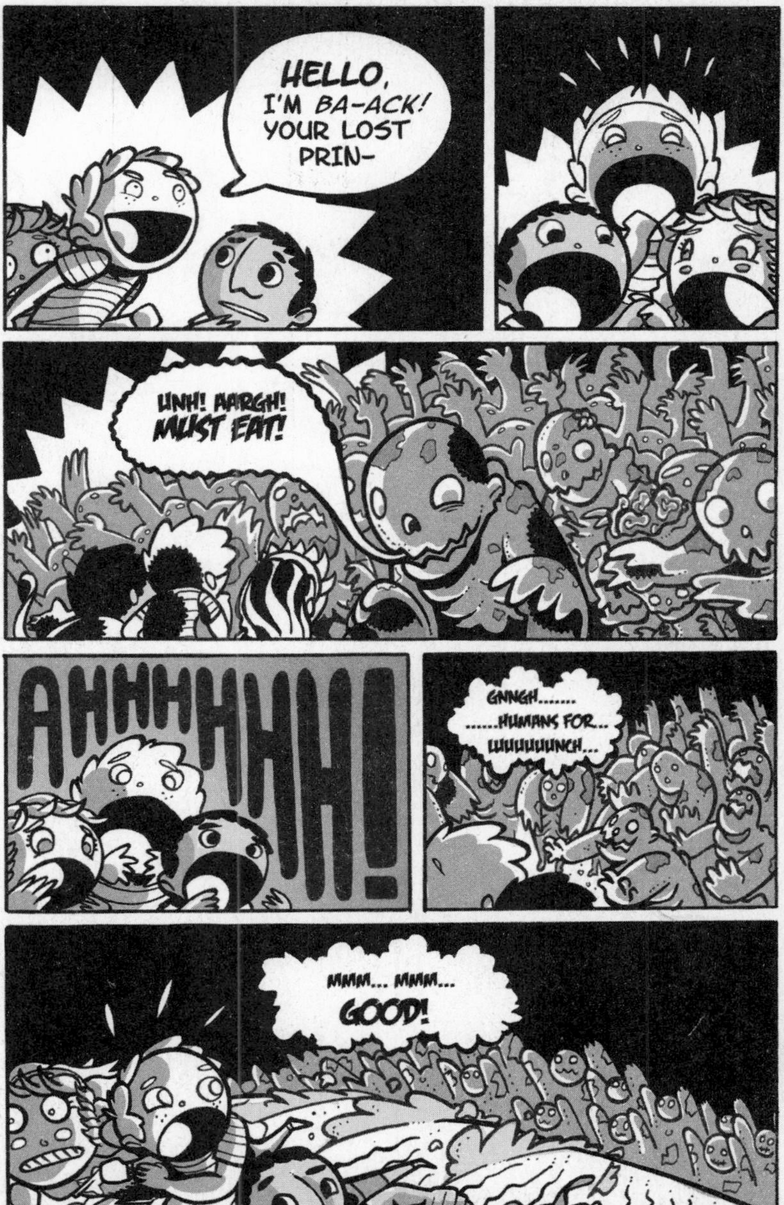
HELLO, I'M BA-ACK! YOUR LOST PRIN-
UNH! AARGH! MUST EAT!
AHHHHHHH!
GNNGH....... ....HUMANS FOR... LUUUUUUNCH...
MMM... MMM... GOOD!

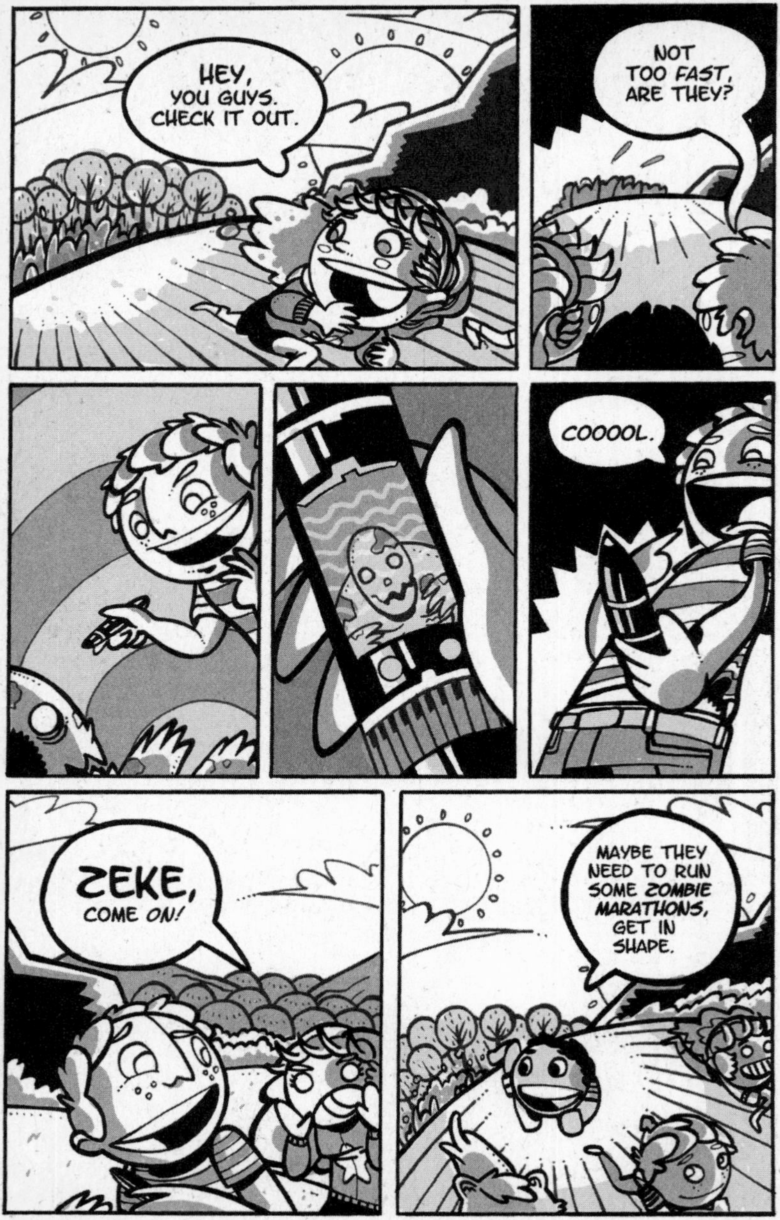
HEY, YOU GUYS. CHECK IT OUT.
NOT TOO FAST, ARE THEY?
COOOOL.
ZEKE, COME ON!
MAYBE THEY NEED TO RUN SOME ZOMBIE MARATHONS, GET IN SHAPE.

THEY'LL NEVER FIND US IN HERE.

YOU SURE WE WON'T GET EATEN, STUMBLING THROUGH THE BRUSH?

UH, I'M SURE.

JUST DON'T GET US LOST.

DON'T WORRY. CATS HAVE A GREAT SENSE OF DIRECTION.

OH, RIGHT. LEAVE IT TO FITZ. HE'LL SAVE US.

LOOK! OUR MEETING PLACE.

A MIRACLE. AND WE DIDN'T EVEN GET DEVOURED BY *DINOSAURS*.

CAN'T YOU BE MORE POSITIVE, FURBALL?

VERY WELL. I'M *POSITIVE* WE DIDN'T GET DEVOURED BY *DINOSAURS*.

WELCOME BACK!

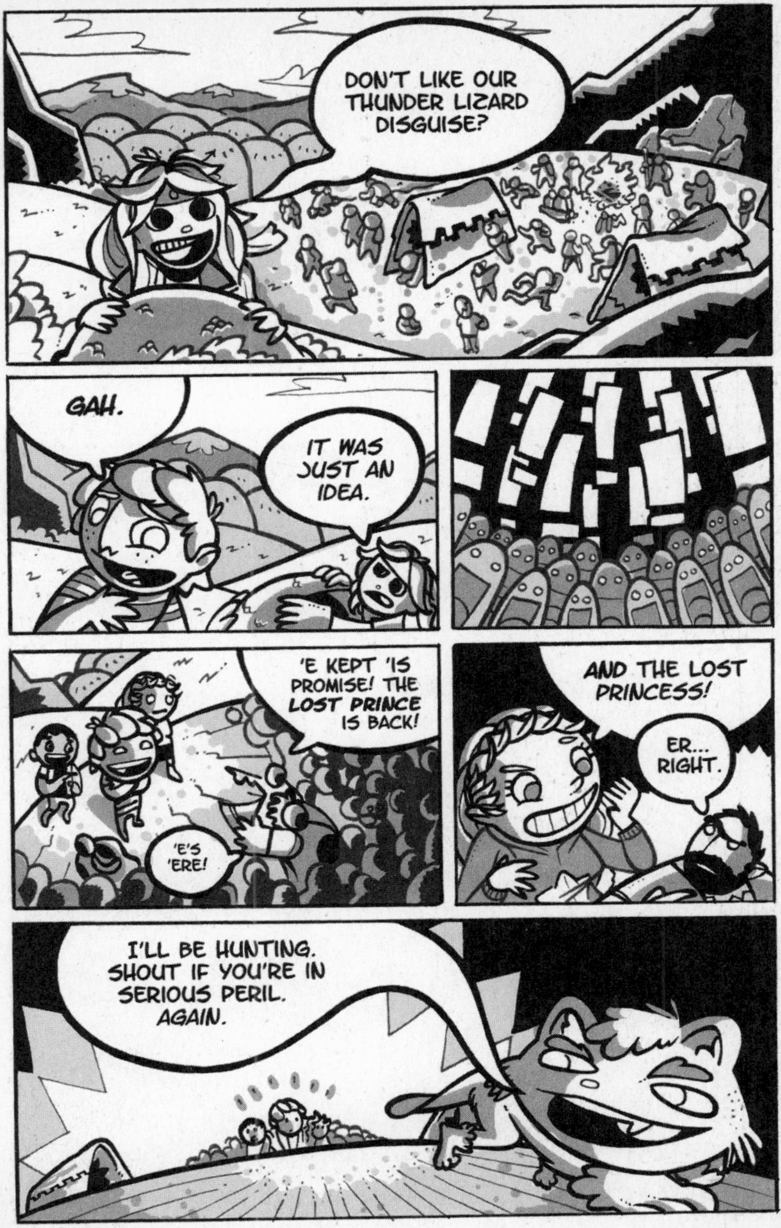
DON'T LIKE OUR THUNDER LIZARD DISGUISE?
GAH.
IT WAS JUST AN IDEA.
'E KEPT 'IS PROMISE! THE LOST PRINCE IS BACK!
'E'S 'ERE!
AND THE LOST PRINCESS!
ER... RIGHT.
I'LL BE HUNTING. SHOUT IF YOU'RE IN SERIOUS PERIL. AGAIN.

DO THEY *HAVE* TO DO THAT?

IT'S A SIGN OF RESPECT.

A LITTLE NOD WOULD DO.

SUIT YOURSELF. BUT TELL US, YOUR ROYAL 'IGHNESS...

ROYAL LOWNESS, MORE LIKE.

'OW WILL WE LIBERATE SKIVVY TOWN? WE AWAIT YOUR INSIGHT.

UH... WELL, THAT IS...

IS THAT *UNDERLORD* GUY GOING TO BE HOME?

NO WORRIES. THE *UNDERLORD'S* UP IN *YOUR* WORLD.

OUR WORLD?

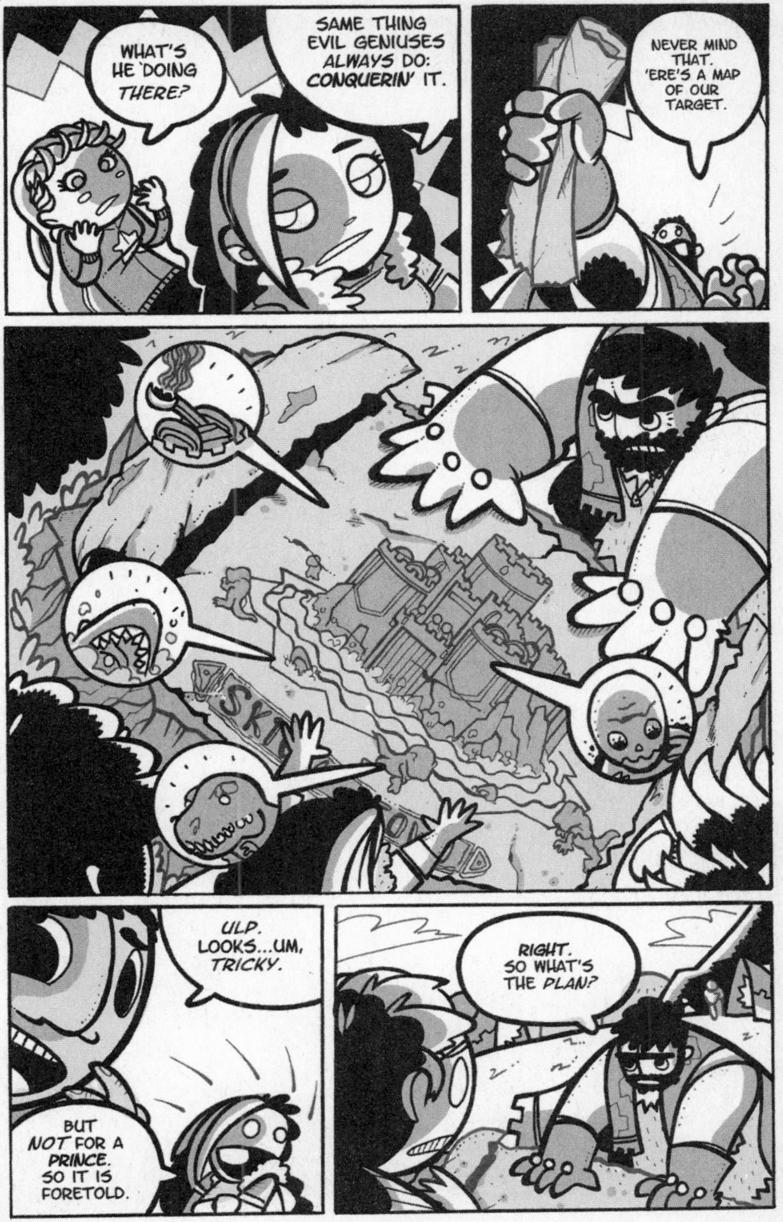

WHAT'S HE 'DOING THERE?
SAME THING EVIL GENIUSES ALWAYS DO: CONQUERIN' IT.
NEVER MIND THAT. 'ERE'S A MAP OF OUR TARGET.
ULP. LOOKS...UM, TRICKY.
BUT NOT FOR A PRINCE. SO IT IS FORETOLD.
RIGHT. SO WHAT'S THE PLAN?

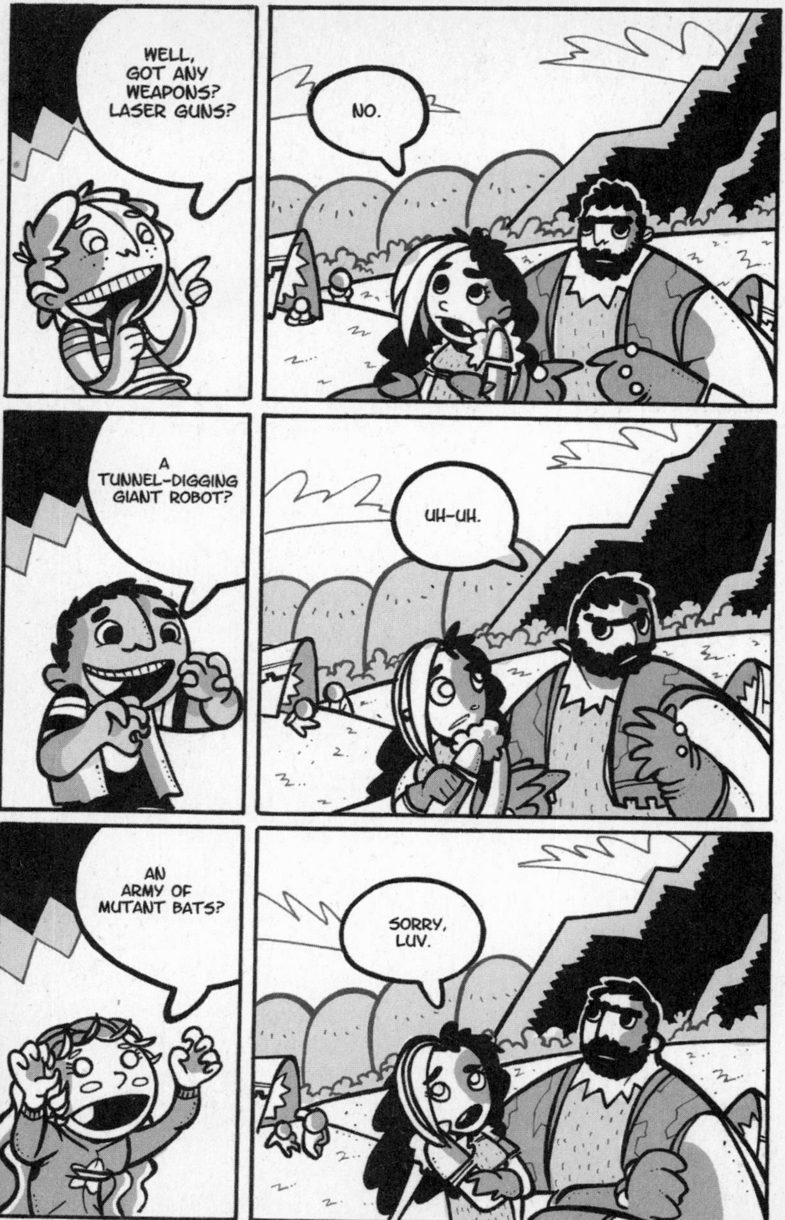
WELL, GOT ANY WEAPONS? LASER GUNS?
NO.
A TUNNEL-DIGGING GIANT ROBOT?
UH-UH.
AN ARMY OF MUTANT BATS?
SORRY, LUV.

UM... THEY HAD A POWER OBJECT IN DUNGHILLS AND DRAGONS. HAVE YOU GOT ONE OF THOSE?

A DUNG 'ILL?

NO, A POWER OBJECT.

WUZZAT?

OH, AN ECHANTED SWORD, A RUBY AMULET...

THE SCEPTER IS GONE.

SO'S THE THRONE AND THE BRUSH.

HMM...

ANYTHING WILL DO, EVEN A HOLY LUMP.

THERE IS AN 'OLY LUMP-- THE GREAT LUMP OF PU.

THERE YOU GO. PROBLEM SOLVED.

MMM, 'ADN'T THOUGHT OF THAT.

'URRAH FOR THE LOST PRINCE!

AND THE LOST HIPPOPOTAMUS WRANGLER!

I THOUGHT YOU WERE THE LOST DIDGERIDOO PLAYER?

I CHANGED MY MIND.

'URRAH!

SO, WHERE DO WE START THE SEARCH?

LOOK AT THE TIME!

WE CAN'T GO AFTER ANY LUMPS OF... WHATEVER. IF WE'RE NOT HOME BY FIVE, QUEEN KONG WILL COME AFTER US.

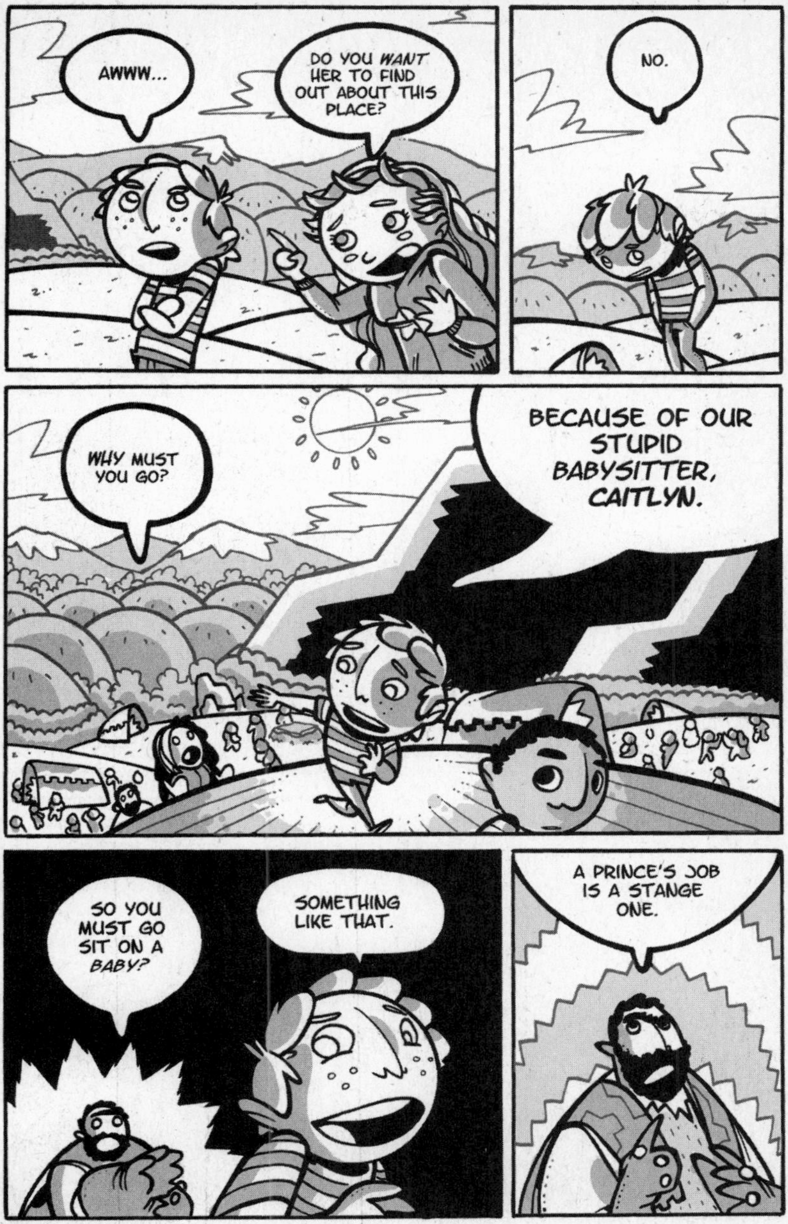
AWWW...
DO YOU WANT HER TO FIND OUT ABOUT THIS PLACE?
NO.
WHY MUST YOU GO?
BECAUSE OF OUR STUPID BABYSITTER, CAITLYN.
SO YOU MUST GO SIT ON A BABY?
SOMETHING LIKE THAT.
A PRINCE'S JOB IS A STANGE ONE.

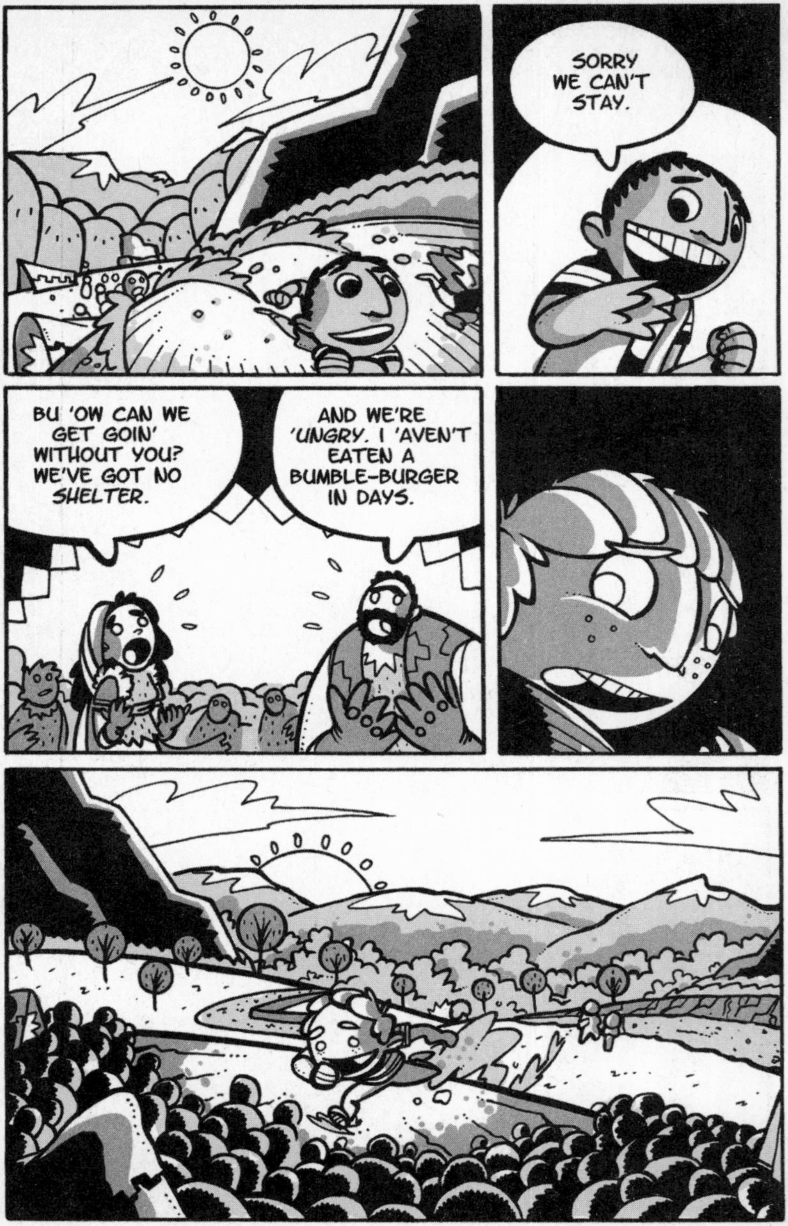
SORRY WE CAN'T STAY.
BU 'OW CAN WE GET GOIN' WITHOUT YOU? WE'VE GOT NO SHELTER.
AND WE'RE 'UNGRY. I 'AVEN'T EATEN A BUMBLE-BURGER IN DAYS.

OKAY, HERE'S THE PLAN. YOU FIND THE POWER OBJECT. WE'LL BE BACK TOMORROW WITH A SCHEME ON HOW TO GET INTO SKIVVY TOWN.

AYE, YOUR SLYNESS.

GOOD LUCK WITH THE WHOLE GREAT LUMP THINGY.

BEWARE THE UNDERLORD!

BUT HOW WILL WE RECOGNIZE HIM?

'E'LL BE THE ONE TAKIN' OVER YOUR WORLD.

OH, GREAT.

Three Threats

We made it back home just after five thirty, safe and sound.

"Where *were* you brats?" yelled Caitlyn as we slipped through the door. "I'm gonna totally *skin* you."

Well, *sound* anyway.

"Sorry," said Steph. "I was trying to get 'em to move, but you know boys."

The little traitor. Luckily, Caitlyn fell for it.

"I know, I know," said Caitlyn. "Can't live with

'em, can't lock 'em up in the zoo."

They giggled. I put up with it.

Then our babysitter dropped the chuckles. "Seriously, that's, like, your absolute last warning. If I let anything happen to you, your parents would totally *kill* me."

"So you'll kill *us* to prevent that?" I said.

Caitlyn shrugged. "It's a paradox, kid." Then her cell phone rang. "Yeah? Oh, *dude*, you wouldn't *believe* what that Weehawken guy said in class. . . ." She wandered off to suck up all the oxygen in the house.

Steph and I hit the family room. I flopped down in front of the TV. She broke out her math assignment.

(Yeah, she's the kind who does homework and chores before anything else. And the sickest part is, she actually likes it.)

I watched the tube and flipped through *The*

Book of Booty that we had brought back from Underwhere. Its pages were crinkly and yellowed. And it stank faintly of rotten eggs. The writing made my brain hurt—even worse than Mrs. Ricotta's story problems.

"Says here that the Scepter can steal souls," I said.

"Uh-huh," said Stephanie. But I could tell she was barely listening.

A commercial blared out. There was that rapper, Beefy D, gold teeth gleaming, face half-hidden behind gigantic sunglasses.

"Yo, yo, padangle!" he yelled. "Get your angle in the hangle. Think ya can rap? Come open up your trap."

As he began to rap, the music and backup singers totally drowned him out. An announcer's voice cut in.

"I'm no rapper," I said. "But this guy sounds pretty lame."

"*Mm-hm*," said Steph.

Before I could change the channel, our phone jangled. *Ring, ring!*

I picked it up. "Hello?"

"Is this the Underhill residence?" a deep voice rumbled.

"Yeah."

"May I speak with your mother or father? It's most urgent."

I looked over at Steph. "They, uh, can't come to the phone," I said.

"I'm Dr. J. Robert Prufrock," he said. "A friend of your great-aunt Zenobia's. I need to know something very important. Did your aunt leave you anything?"

I thought, *Well, what's the harm?* "We got a beat-up trunk," I said, "a letter, and some dusty old junk."

Steph looked up at me and wrinkled her forehead.

"I believe that something she brought back from our last expedition is, well, magical," said Dr. Prufrock. "And highly dangerous."

"Dangerous?" I echoed.

Holy crud! Did this guy know about Underwhere?

Stephanie got up and joined me. I twisted the receiver so she could hear.

"We, er, *collected* several items, and now all manner of strange things are happening," he said. "Electrical disturbances, mutated animals . . ."

"Like butt-birds?" I said, thinking of Fitz's road-kill treats.

"Great bumbling Zeus!" boomed Dr. Prufrock. "It's happening to you, too?"

"Yes," said Stephanie. "And you won't believe where we—"

"Listen, children," said the doctor. "You must hide her artifact somewhere safe. I fear that its owner may be looking for what we took, even now. You're in terrible . . ." He fell silent. "Eh?"

"Terrible *eh*?" I said.

"*Shh,*" he said. "There's someone on the street."

"How do we know we can trust you?" said Steph.

"*Which* artifact?" I asked.

"Must go," whispered Dr. Prufrock. "Hide the Throne."

And—*click*—he hung up.

Yeesh.

I stared at the receiver. "Throne?" I said. "What throne?"

On the way to school the next morning, I worried. How could I help the Undies free their city? What would I do for my science project? And was my rap song good enough to keep Melvin from rearranging my face?

A long silver car pulled up to the curb. Out stepped the spies.

Great. One more thing to worry about.

Agent Belly scratched his fake nose. "Let's hear your report. It better be good."

Steph and I told them about our latest trip to Underwhere—but not that I was the lost prince. I downloaded my spy camera shots onto their laptop computer.

"Zombies," said Agent Mole. "Little people."

They traded a long look. Mole's hairy mole twitched with joy.

"Uh-huh," said Belly. "With this evidence, our project—"

Agent Mole drew a finger across his throat, and Agent Belly stopped cold.

"So if you guys are happy," I said, "we'll stop spying now."

Agent Belly smiled. "Not quite. Your parents

are scheduled to return from a dig, um . . ." He snapped his fingers.

"Next week," said Mole.

"It would be such a shame if they didn't come back."

Ulp.

"Wh-what do you mean?" I asked, trying to steady my voice.

"So much danger at a dig," said Agent Belly. "Infected trowels . . ."

"Porta Potti accidents," said Mole.

My shoulders slumped. Steph bit her lip.

"Keep up the good work, kids," said Agent Belly as they piled into the car.

"For how long?" said Stephanie.

Agent Mole's sunglasses stared blankly at us. "As long as it takes."

And they drove off in a cloud of thick bluish smoke.

Bad Is Good

All through our history lesson, I was distracted. I kept sneaking glances at Melvin, knowing he'd corner me at recess. And I wasn't looking forward to our chat.

Then Mrs. Ricotta said something that grabbed my attention.

"Let's talk about Greek history," she said.

That wasn't it.

"Does anyone know how the Greeks conquered the city of Troy?"

That was it.

Nobody raised a hand, so our teacher told us about the Trojan Horse. It seems the Greek army hid some soldiers inside a giant wooden horse and gave it to the Trojans. The Trojans brought the horse inside Troy. Then the Greek guys sneaked out, opened the gates for their army, and conquered the city.

Bingo. Who knew history could be useful?

All the Undies had to do was build some kind of Trojan Horse thingie. Then they could sneak it into Skivvy Town. And I thought I knew just what kind of thingie the Undies would like.

I started sketching. By break time, my design was complete.

Watch out, Skivvy Town. Here comes the lost prince.

At recess, Hector and I kicked a soccer ball while I told him the latest news.

"You're supposed to hide your aunt's *what*?" he asked.

"Throne," I said. "If we can even find one."

"O-kay . . ."

I popped the ball up and bounced it off my head. "And this Prufrock guy might—*ow!*—know about Underwhere. But I don't know if we can believe him. He sounded pretty nutty."

"About one Froot Loop shy of a full box," said Hector.

We cracked up. My crooked kick spun the ball off to the side.

Thoomp. The custodian caught it.

"Oh, Mr. Wheener," said Hector. "Can we have our ball back?"

"It's *Veener*," growled the shaggy-haired janitor. "And be careful. Someone could get hurt."

He tossed the ball with a dark look, and dragged his trash bag away.

"Where did *he* come from?" I asked.

"Dunno," said Hector. "But here comes some more."

I spun. Melvin Prang and Darryl were headed straight for us.

Too late to run.

"Yo, padangle!" said Melvin. "What's the hangle?"

"Uh, hey, Melvin," I said.

He strutted right up to me. Darryl took my other side.

"Got my rap, runt?" said the bully.

I gulped. "Yeah. It's um, a rough draft." I fished the paper from my pocket.

Lips moving, Melvin read my lines. His frown deepened.

Uh-oh.

He looked up. "It's bad," he said.

"Sorry. I can try—"

Darryl interrupted. "*Bad* is good, dweeb."

"That's Beefy D's motto," said Melvin. "Bad is good, and evil is awesome."

I blinked. "That's nice—uh, I mean, wicked."

He stuffed my lame rap in his pocket. "Stay cool, fool." Melvin shoved me.

I staggered, off balance. Mean and Meaner strolled off.

"I can't believe he went for those lyrics," I said.

"Stinkeroo?" asked Hector.

"Yeah," I said. "Sometimes, bad is *bad*."

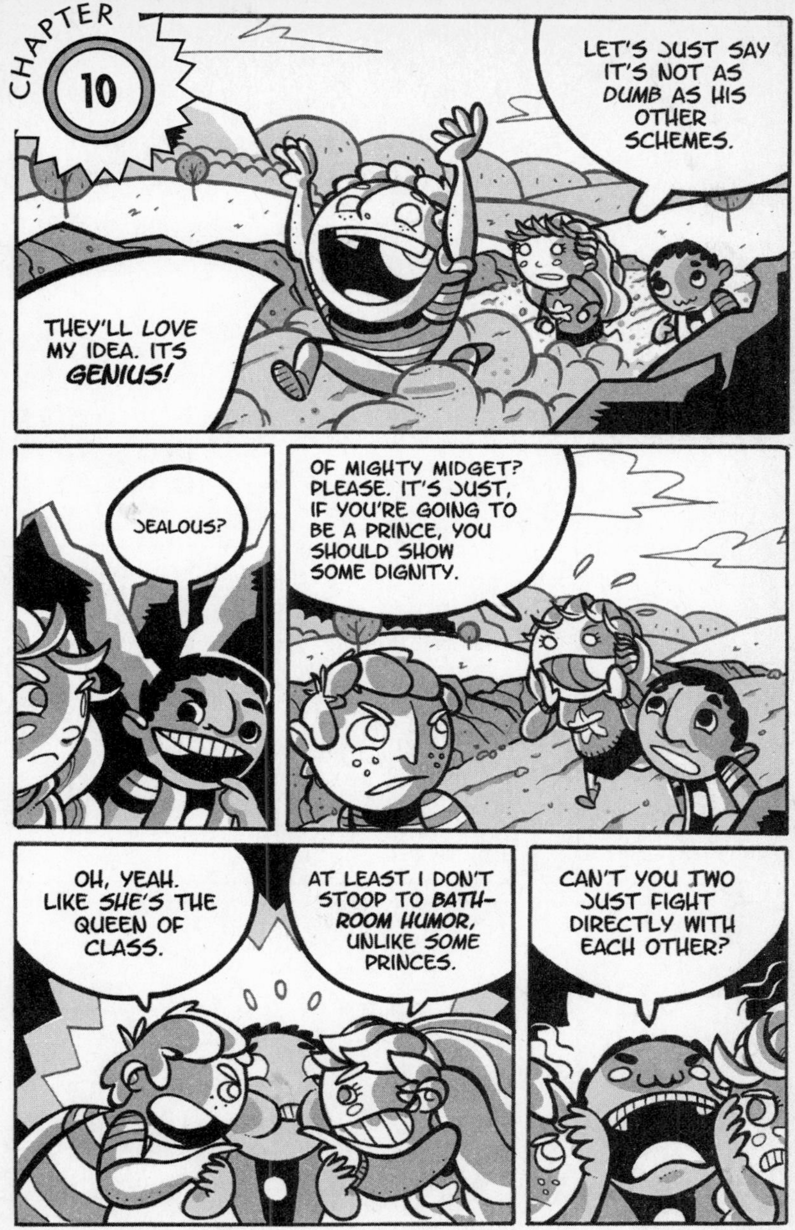
CHAPTER 10
LET'S JUST SAY IT'S NOT AS DUMB AS HIS OTHER SCHEMES.
THEY'LL LOVE MY IDEA. ITS *GENIUS!*
JEALOUS?
OF MIGHTY MIDGET? PLEASE. IT'S JUST, IF YOU'RE GOING TO BE A PRINCE, YOU SHOULD SHOW SOME DIGNITY.
OH, YEAH. LIKE *SHE'S* THE QUEEN OF CLASS.
AT LEAST I DON'T STOOP TO *BATHROOM HUMOR,* UNLIKE SOME PRINCES.
CAN'T YOU TWO JUST FIGHT DIRECTLY WITH EACH OTHER?

CAN WE JUST STOP WITH THE *MOONING*, GUYS? I'VE GOT A *GREAT IDEA!*

'ULLO, YOUR WORSHIP. IS IT AS GOOD AS THE 'OLY LUMP?

WHY? DIDN'T THAT WORK?

TURNS OUT, THE GREAT LUMP OF PU BELONGS TO A GRUMPY TROLL, NAME OF *MIMI TWALETTE.*

AH.

AND MIMI DIDN' TAKE *KINDLY* TO US TRYIN' TO STEAL 'ER LUMP.

OH. I GUESS THAT'S WHY YOU GUYS AREN'T ALL *FLUSHED* WITH VICTORY. HEH HEH HEH.

HEH.

DON'T WORRY. THIS NEW PLAN IS *MUCH* BETTER.

IT BETTER BE.

DO YOU UNDIES HAVE A *GARBAGE DUMP?*

'COURSE WE DO.

DOES IT *STINK?*

TO 'IGH 'EAVEN.

PERFECT.

THE ROTTEN BANANA EXPERIMENT — BUT *BIG - TIME*

WHAT DO YOU 'AVE IN MIND?

WE'LL NEED BELLOWS, AND JARS, AND...

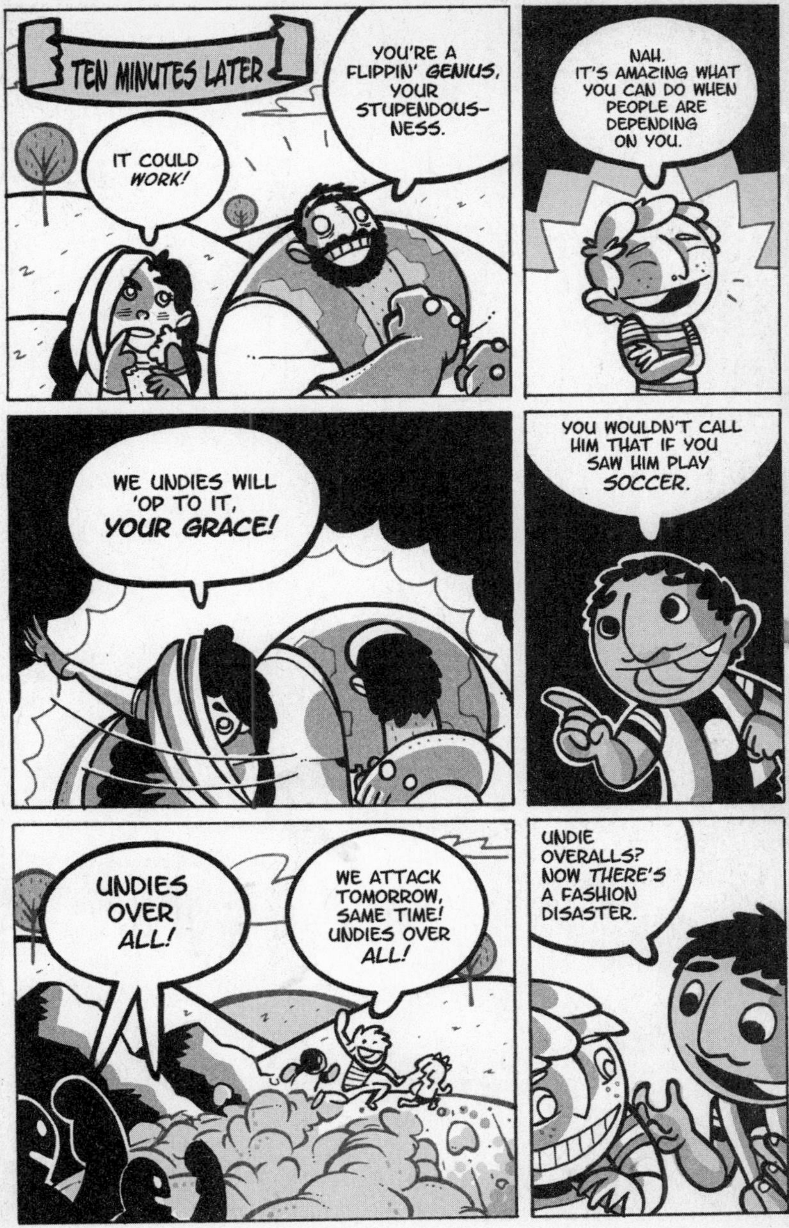
TEN MINUTES LATER
IT COULD WORK!
YOU'RE A FLIPPIN' GENIUS, YOUR STUPENDOUSNESS.
NAH. IT'S AMAZING WHAT YOU CAN DO WHEN PEOPLE ARE DEPENDING ON YOU.
WE UNDIES WILL 'OP TO IT, YOUR GRACE!
YOU WOULDN'T CALL HIM THAT IF YOU SAW HIM PLAY SOCCER.
UNDIES OVER ALL!
WE ATTACK TOMORROW, SAME TIME! UNDIES OVER ALL!
UNDIE OVERALLS? NOW THERE'S A FASHION DISASTER.

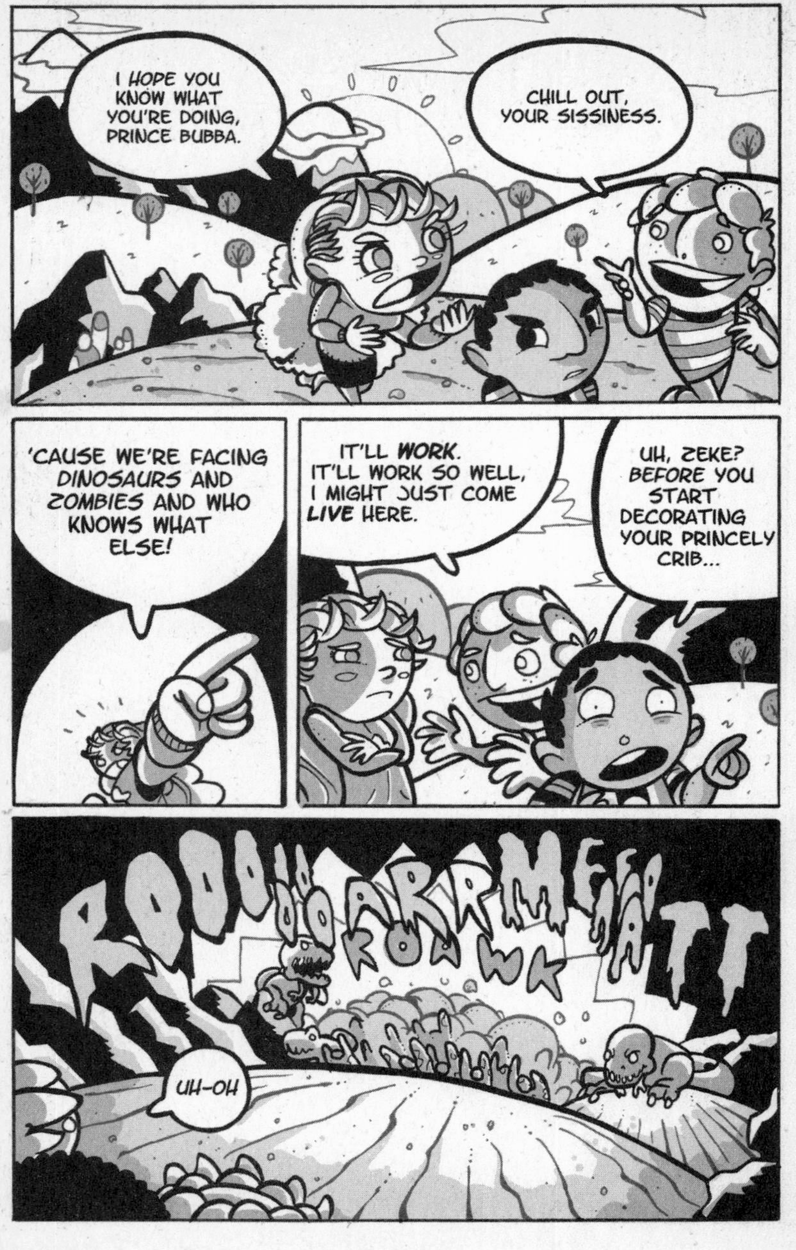
I HOPE YOU KNOW WHAT YOU'RE DOING, PRINCE BUBBA.
CHILL OUT, YOUR SISSINESS.
'CAUSE WE'RE FACING DINOSAURS AND ZOMBIES AND WHO KNOWS WHAT ELSE!
IT'LL WORK. IT'LL WORK SO WELL, I MIGHT JUST COME LIVE HERE.
UH, ZEKE? BEFORE YOU START DECORATING YOUR PRINCELY CRIB...
UH-OH

YIKES!.

MOAAAN

BEHIND US!

WHAT'LL WE DO?

I HAVE AN IDEA. SEE HOW THE ZOMBIES AND DINOS DON'T ATTACK EACH OTHER?

YES. SO?

IF WE ACT LIKE THEM, THEY'LL LEAVE US ALONE.

SORRY, I LEFT MY STEGOSAURUS COSTUME AT HOME.

NOT DINOS, DUMMY. ZOMBIES. WATCH.

RIIP! RIPP!

RUSSLE TUSSLE

...MUST... ...FIND... MISSING LEG.

VERY CONVINCING.

IT'LL NEVER WORK.

YOU GOT A *BETTER* IDEA? THEY'RE GETTING CLOSER.

OH, ALL *RIGHT*. BUT I'M NOT PUTTING DIRT IN MY HAIR.

FUSSLE

BUSSLE

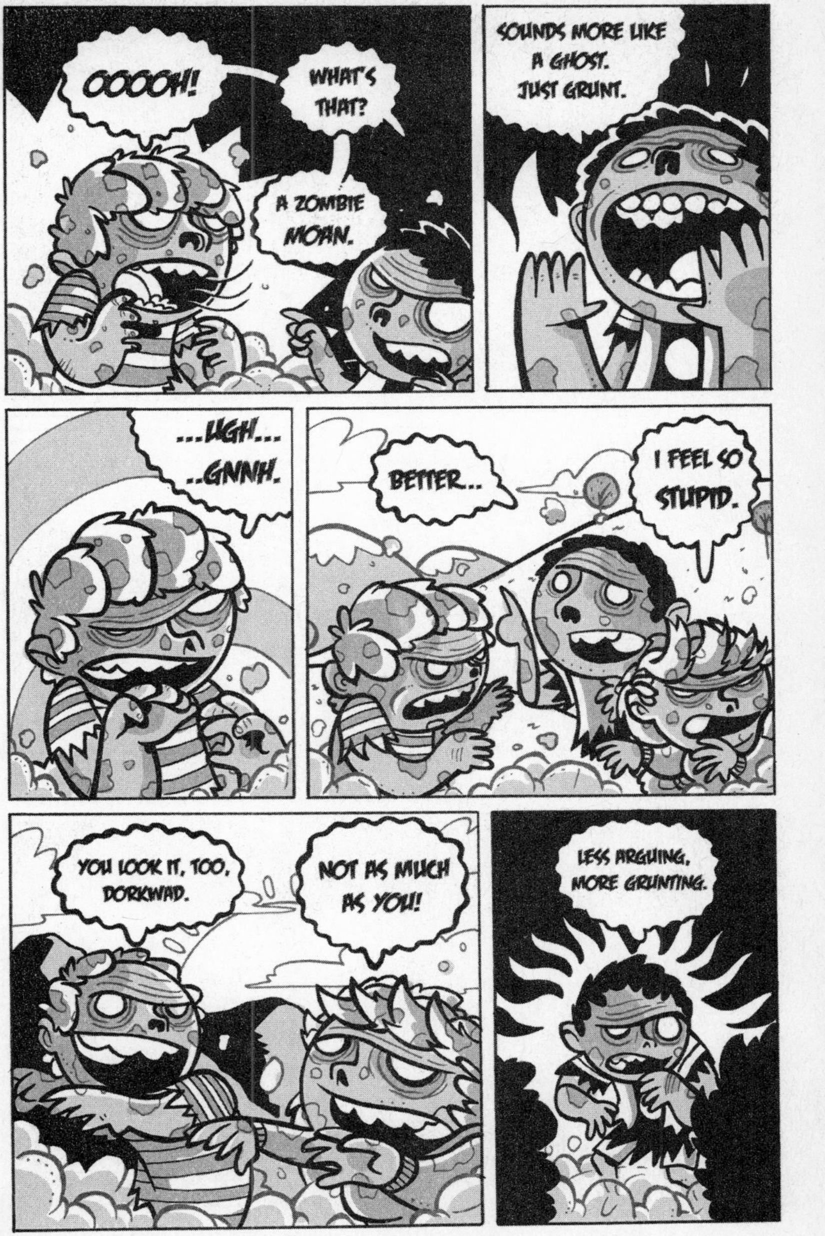
OOOOH!
WHAT'S THAT?
A ZOMBIE MOAN.
SOUNDS MORE LIKE A GHOST. JUST GRUNT.
...UGH... ..GNNH.
BETTER...
I FEEL SO STUPID.
YOU LOOK IT, TOO, DORKWAD.
NOT AS MUCH AS YOU!
LESS ARGUING, MORE GRUNTING.

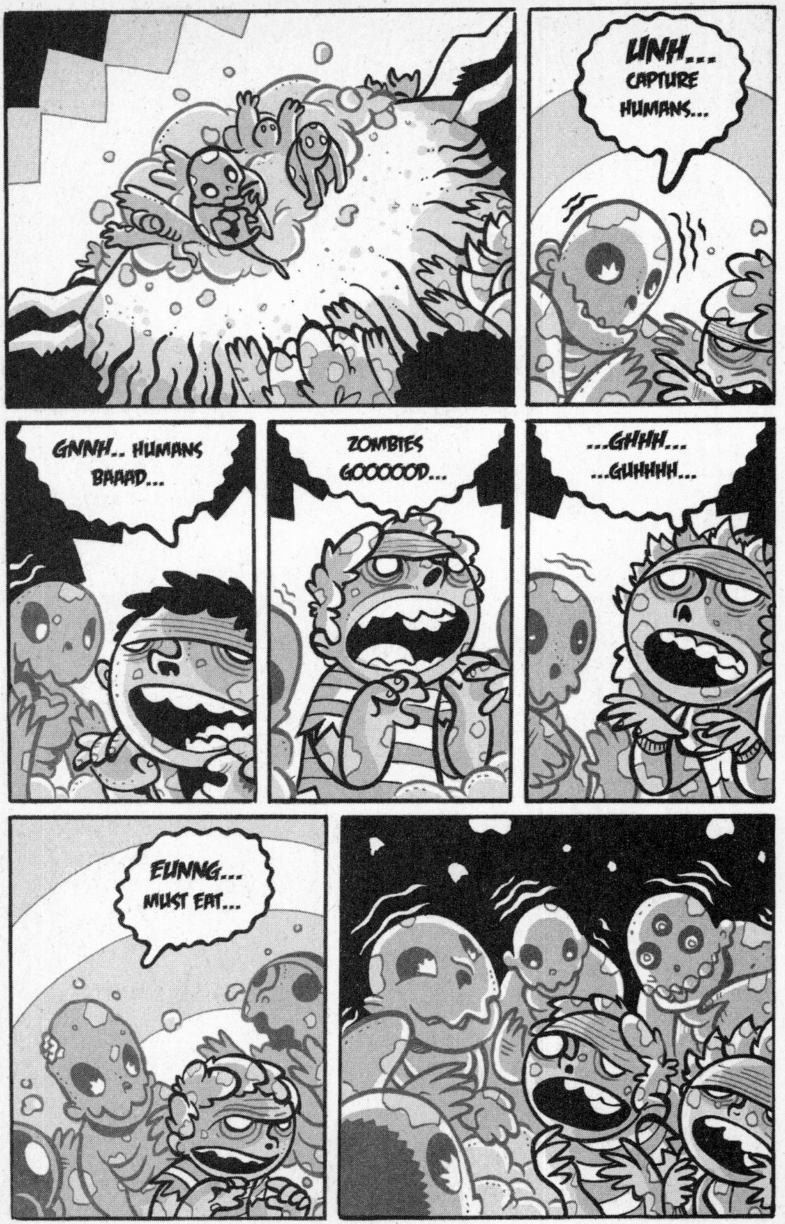
UNH... CAPTURE HUMANS...
GNNH.. HUMANS BAAAD...
ZOMBIES GOOOOOD...
...GHHH... ...GUHHHH...
EUNNG... MUST EAT...

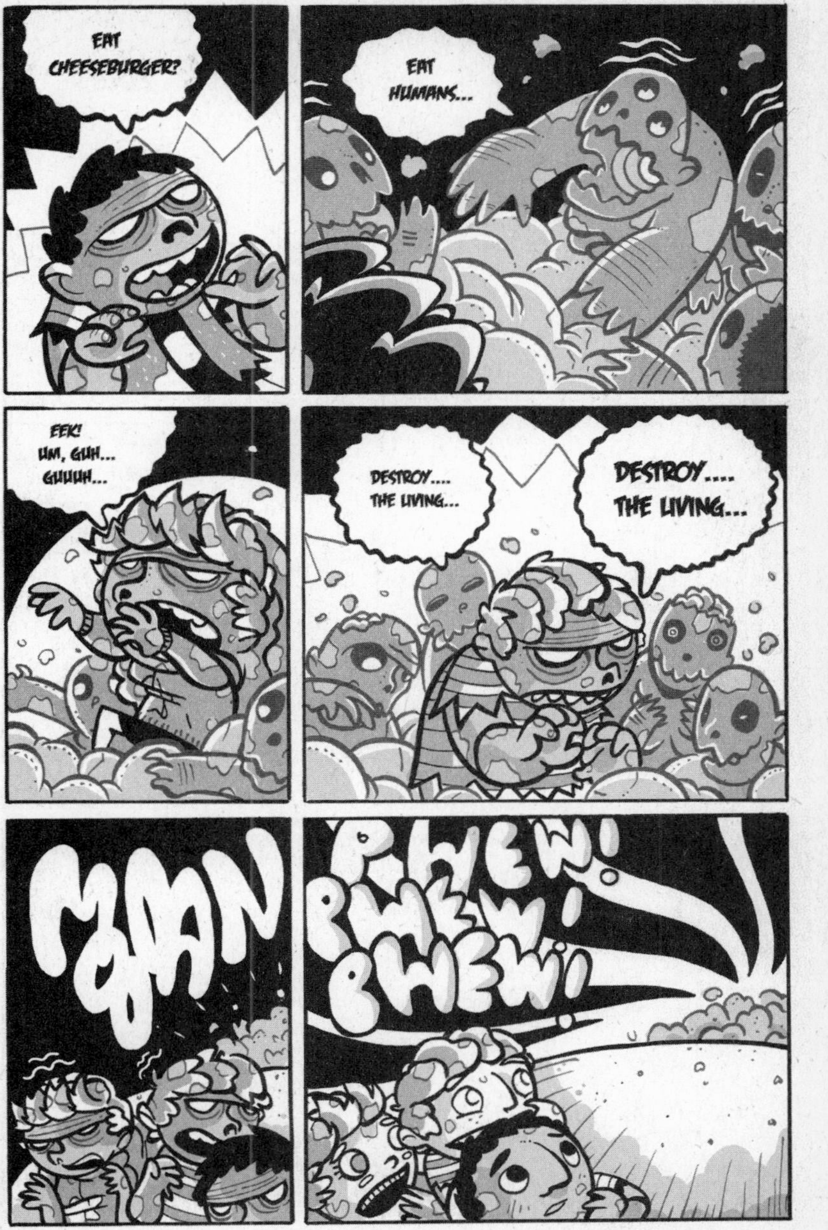
EAT CHEESEBURGER?
EAT HUMANS...
EEK! UM, GUH... GUUUH...
DESTROY.... THE LIVING...
DESTROY.... THE LIVING...
ZAAN
PHEW! PHEW! PHEW!

LET'S GO!

REMEMBER WHAT I SAID ABOUT MAYBE *MOVING* TO UNDER-WHERE?

YES?

NEXT TIME I SAY THAT, *BOP* ME ON THE HEAD.

I THOUGHT YOU'D *NEVER* ASK!

CHAPTER 11

Beefing Up

Back at home, a surprise was waiting: a familiar black stretch Humvee parked in front of our house.

"It's that same car," said Stephanie. "Who could it be?"

"A movie star?" said Hector.

"Yeah," I said. "Hollywood wants to do my life story."

Steph tossed her curls. "Don't be silly. They're not visiting us."

But when we opened the front door, a bigger surprise sat on our couch.

"Yo, yo, yo, pahangle," said the rapper Beefy D. "What's the dwangle?"

I stared. "Huh?" was all I could say.

Beefy D spread out on the sofa with huge bodyguards on either side. Gold teeth twinkled in his smile, and he wore purple jockey shorts over his pants.

"Look who dropped in!" squealed Caitlyn. She perched on the armchair, grinning madly. Queen Kong had had a personality transplant. "It's Beefy D himself!"

The rapper raised his fist. "Word," he said.

"Uh, *kumquat*?" I said.

Caitlyn glared.

"What?" I said. "*Kumquat* isn't a word?"

"Beefy D wants to ask us something important," she said.

The rapper leaned forward. He was built short and wide, like a mini refrigerator. "Yo, come be mah pahangles on mah shwangle. Wanna hangle?"

I looked at Steph and Hector. They were frowning, too.

"Huh?" said Stephanie.

Caitlyn rolled her eyes. "What's your major malfunction? He wants us to, like, be his guests at his store opening tomorrow night!"

Beefy D nodded. "Indeedy-dangle," he said.

"Isn't that, like, *megacool*?" Caitlyn gushed.

"I guess," I said.

"Why us?" said Steph.

Our cousin stood. "He's chosen one family at random to, like, be on his show. And out of all the families in town, he picked *us*!"

"*How* us?" I said.

"I've already accepted for everyone," said

109

Caitlyn. "Hector, too."

Hector shrugged. "Okay. Us."

Beefy D beamed. His smile looked like a jewelry store window. "Truly evil, mah pahangles," he said.

"Truly evil," echoed his bodyguards.

To our blank looks, Caitlyn said, "*Evil* means awesome."

"I knew that," I said.

"Word," said the rapper. "It's a dehangle." He hopped off the couch, and just came up to his guards' bellybuttons. I'm short, but this guy was *short*.

He strutted around the living room. "Say, where's the loo, baboo? This dudangle's gotta pangle."

"The *loo*?" asked Stephanie.

"Your poopangle, your jangle, your *throne*. Knowhutahmsayin'?"

"Oh," said Caitlyn. "The bathroom's this way."

She led Beefy D and his beefier bodyguards into the hall.

"Our *throne*?" I wondered. "Dr. Prufrock mentioned a throne. . . ."

"That weird toilet in your dad's office?" said Hector.

"It does look kinda thronelike. But who'd sit on it—King Putt?"

We laughed.

"Very princely," said Steph. "Anyway, I bet it's just a coincidence."

Even so, I crossed the room to watch. Beefy's guys stood talking to Caitlyn in the hall. The bathroom door was closed.

Hector joined me. "What's up?" he asked.

"I'm not sure," I said. "But something's weird about that guy."

"Whut the heckangle do ya mean, pahangle?"

"Exactly."

Soon, Beefy D appeared, wiping his hands on his sparkly gold shirt. He drifted toward us, then poked his nose into Dad's workroom.

"That's my uncle's office," said Caitlyn.

I stepped forward and reached past him. "Yeah, and it's off-limits," I said, shutting the door.

Beefy D backed into the hall. He waved a ring-covered hand. "That's all Kool-and-the-Gangle, pahangle," he said.

Up close, he smelled of rotten eggs and fruity aftershave. *Yeesh.* And his fishy white face seemed to have a faint blue halo.

Beefy D noticed my stare. For a second, his features froze.

Then, he flashed that million-dollar grin. "Check *me* out. I'm purty as a pichangle." Beefy D laughed, and his guards laughed along. They brushed past.

At the front door, the rapper turned. "Laters,

pahangles. Gonna send the limosangle tomorra."
He made a V with his fingers. "Peas and carrots."

The door closed behind them with a *thunk*.

"Omigod, *omigod*!" squealed Caitlyn, whipping out her cell phone. "Brittany will *die* and come back to life when she hears this!" She retreated to her room.

From the window, I watched Beefy D and his crew walk to the Humvee.

Hector patted my shoulder. "Cheer up. There are worse things than being at Beefy D's opening."

"Yeah," I said. "Sharing an elevator with him. Have you *smelled* the guy?"

At school the next day, everyone was buzzing about Beefy D. The classroom loudspeaker gave us the latest.

"Attention, students," crackled a voice. It was

our principal, Ms. Johnson. "Time to announce the winner of our school rap contest."

Melvin Prang shot me a hard look. "Me," he muttered. "Or else."

"First," said Ms. Johnson, "I want you to know that you are *all* winners. Even if you're not all going to Beefy—uh, Mr. D's show."

Why do grown-ups always say that? *Duh*, we know we're not all winners.

"Yeah, yeah," said Melvin. "Enough about the losers."

"The winner is . . ."

I crossed my fingers.

"Melvin Prang?" Ms. Johnson said, trying to hide her surprise. "Uh, congratulations, Melvin."

The class gave a halfhearted cheer.

Sheesh. I felt confused.

My rap was cool enough to win the contest. That was good.

But it meant Melvin and I would be at the same event. That was bad.

Confusion was replaced by worry.

"I hope you haven't forgotten," said our teacher, Mrs. Ricotta. "Your science projects are due tomorrow."

How could I forget? Half my grade depended on it. And with all the interruptions, I hadn't even started yet.

Maybe I'd get lucky. Maybe the zombies would eat me first.

After school, Stephanie started toward the nearby strip mall.

"Wrong way, Steph," I said. "Home is *that* direction."

"But the drugstore is over *here*," she said.

"Why go there?" asked Hector.

"Need some Pepto-Bismol 'cause you're sick

with jealousy?" I said.

She turned to Hector. "Dwarf Boy's plan includes methane gas, right?"

"Right," he said.

"Have you ever *smelled* methane? We need surgical masks for protection."

"Oh," I said. "I hadn't thought of that."

Hector grinned. "So what you're saying is, his plan stinks?"

We bought the masks and rushed home. Somehow, we had to help the Undies storm Skivvy Town and return in time for Beefy D's store opening. But as if that wasn't enough . . .

"Zeke," said Steph, as we hit the driveway, "about that weird toilet. . . ." She frowned. "Maybe we should hide it. Just in case."

Hector's grandmother gave us a funny look when we carried the antique potty into his house.

"We've already got one of those," she said.

"It's just for a little while," said Hector. "To keep it safe."

"Safe from what?" asked his grandmother.

"Uh, toilet thieves?" said Hector.

Countdown to a Castle Raid

We stashed Great-aunt Zenobia's toilet in Hector's room. Then, *zip!*—back to my house. After tossing the surgical masks into a book bag, we headed out.

"Don't forget," yelled Caitlyn from the couch. "We leave at, like, six o'clock *sharp*! I'll *murder* you if you zimwats make me miss this. And it won't be the warm and fuzzy kind of murder, either."

"We'll be here," said Steph. And we took off running.

Fitz appeared from nowhere and joined us. But before we could reach the construction site, a familiar silver car pulled up. A window whirred down.

Fitz hissed.

"We've been waiting for your report," said Agent Belly. "Why no call?"

"Uh, we've been busy," I said, fidgeting.

"Do tell," said Mole.

"Not much *to* tell," said Steph. "The Undies have welcomed us."

"The UnderLord has come to conquer our world," I said.

"And my cat can talk English down there," said Hector.

Agent Belly stared at me. "Run that second one by us again?" he said.

Time was short, but we reported what the Undies had said.

"Does this UnderLord have any special powers?" asked Agent Belly.

"Some magic, maybe," I said. "We haven't really met."

Mole's mole twitched. "Magic." He turned to Belly. "That's . . ."

"Exactly," said the chubby agent. "Children, we want you to bring back something magical—a wand, crystal ball, whatever."

"How are we supposed to find—," Stephanie began.

But the window whirred back up, and they motored off.

"Meer *mrrrrr*," Fitz growled.

"You *said* it," said Steph. "I'm *sick* of those guys."

"Me too," I said. "But we'll have to worry about them later."

"Why?"

I shouldered the book bag. "Right now we've got zombies to battle and a castle to storm."

"Oh, that," said Hector. "I knew I was forgetting something."

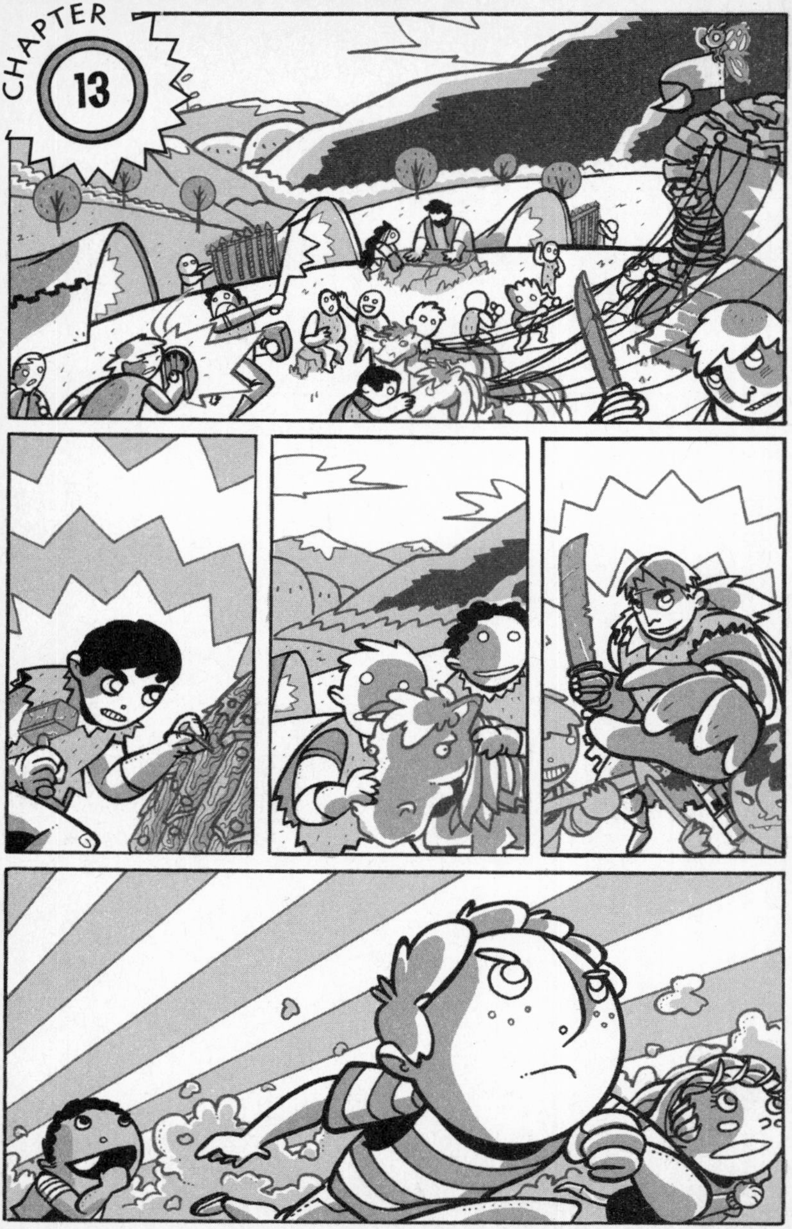
CHAPTER 13

'ERE THEY ARE!

YOUR GRACE! WE WERE AFRAID YOU'D 'AD *SECOND* THOUGHTS.

NO, JUST A SECOND-RATE SENSE OF *DIRECTION*. LUCKILY, THERE WAS A *FELINE* ALONG.

TELL EVERYONE RIDING INSIDE TO WEAR *THESE*.

NEW UPLANDER FASHION?

YOU MIGHT SAY THAT.

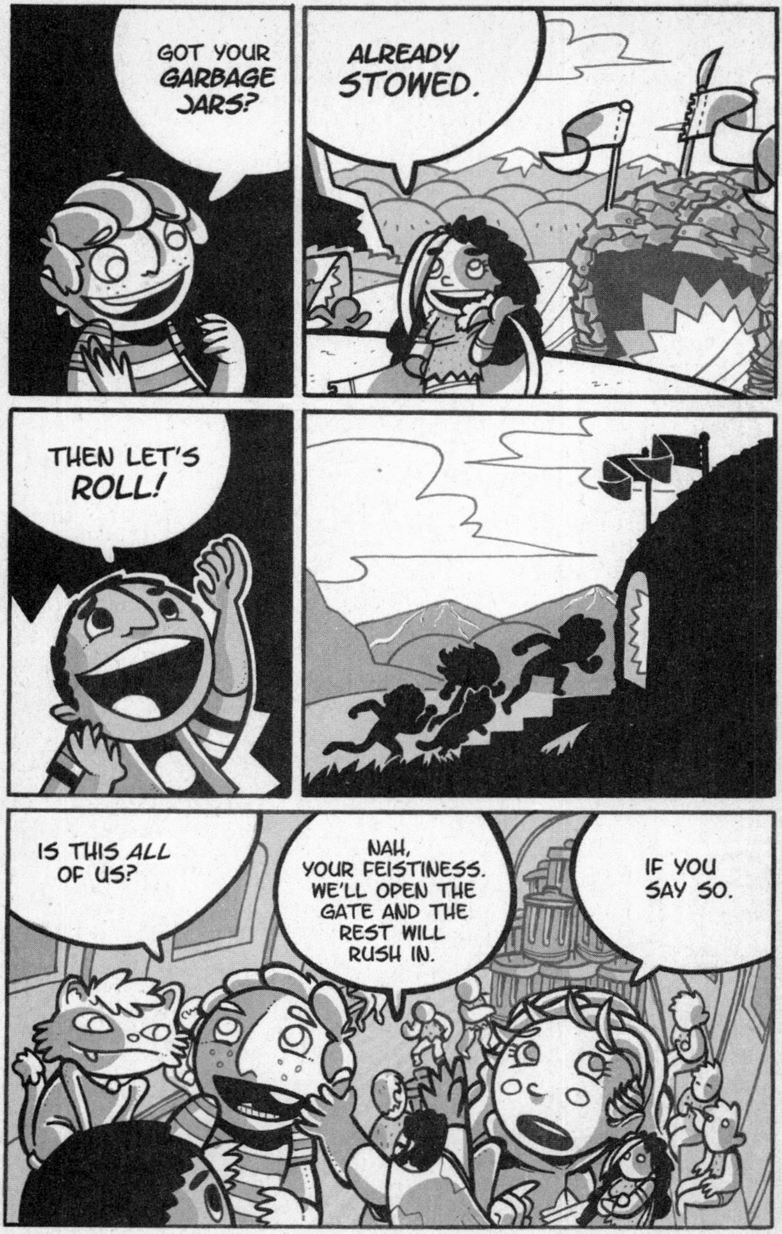
GOT YOUR GARBAGE JARS?
ALREADY STOWED.
THEN LET'S ROLL!
IS THIS ALL OF US?
NAH, YOUR FEISTINESS. WE'LL OPEN THE GATE AND THE REST WILL RUSH IN.
IF YOU SAY SO.

SLAM!

LET'S GO!

CREEK

WOO-HOO!

RUMBLE RUMBLE

ZEKE, IF WE GET KILLED, I'LL NEVER FORGIVE YOU.

CHEER UP, PRINCESS.

HE CALLED ME PRINCESS.

HEAVEN KNOWS YOU *ACT* LIKE ONE.

SO WHAT ARE WE UP AGAINST?

MOSTLY SOLDIERS. A FEW ZOMBIES.

OH, IS THAT ALL?

JUST WAIT TILL THEY SEE US!

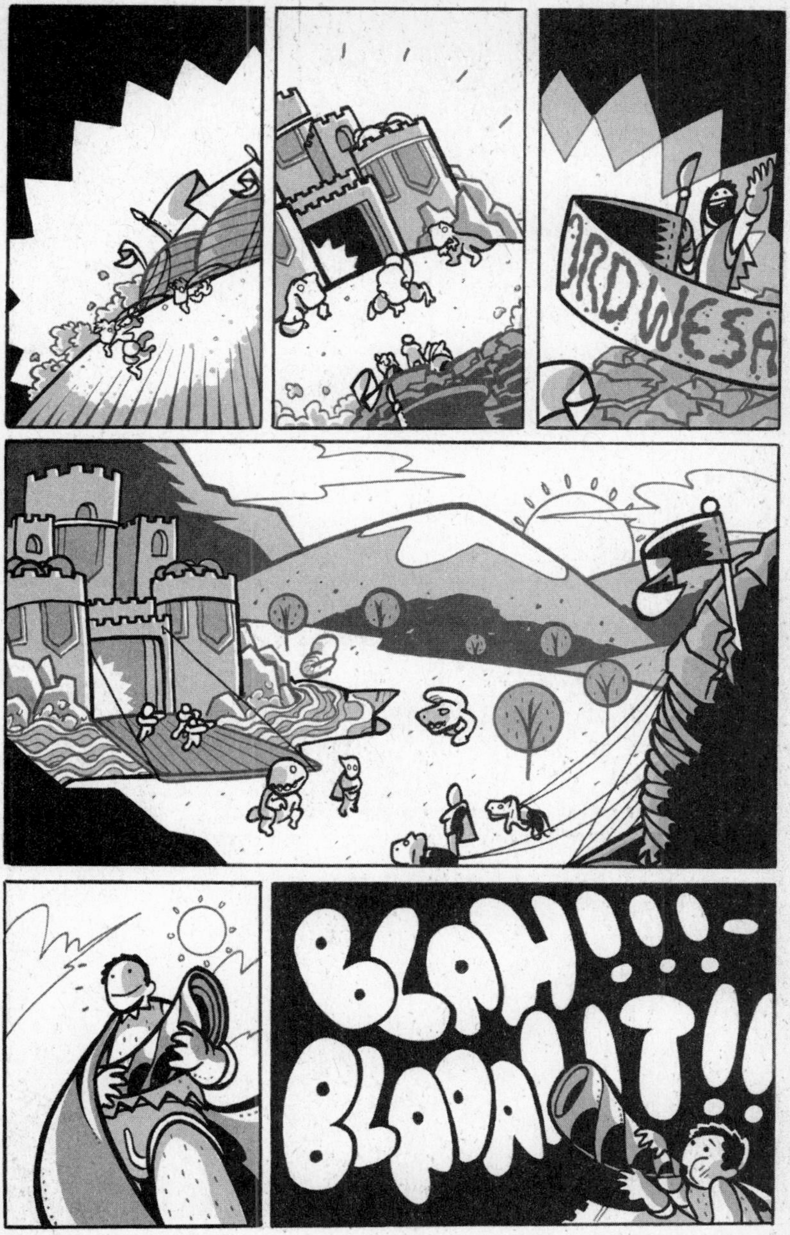
ORDWESA
BLAH!!!-
BLAAAT!!!

BIRTHDAY GIFT FOR THE UNDERLORD! SIGN 'ERE.

ALL YOURS, SQUIRE.

UNH! HEAVIEST BUNS I'VE EVER HAULED.

BIGGEST, TOO.

YOU *THREE,* STAND GUARD. IT'S FOR HIS EVILNESS.

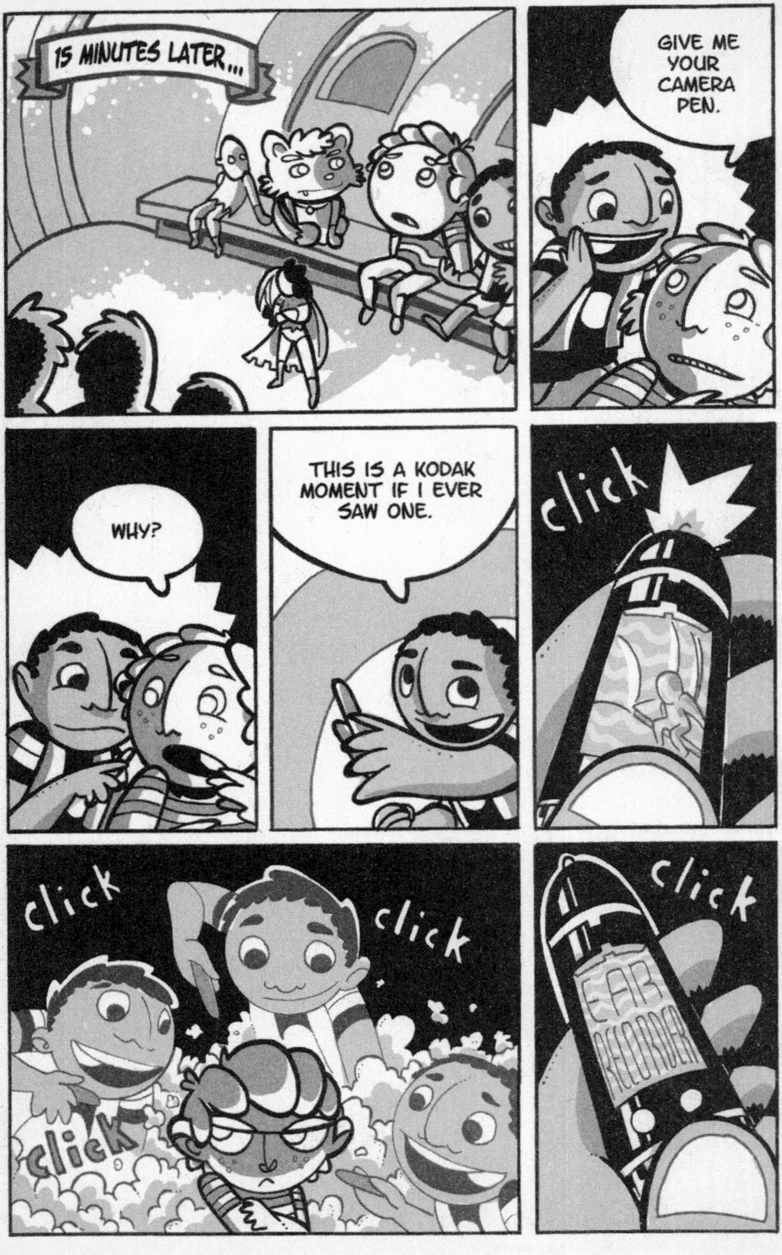

15 MINUTES LATER...
GIVE ME YOUR CAMERA PEN.
WHY?
THIS IS A KODAK MOMENT IF I EVER SAW ONE.
click
click
click
click
click
EAR RECORDER

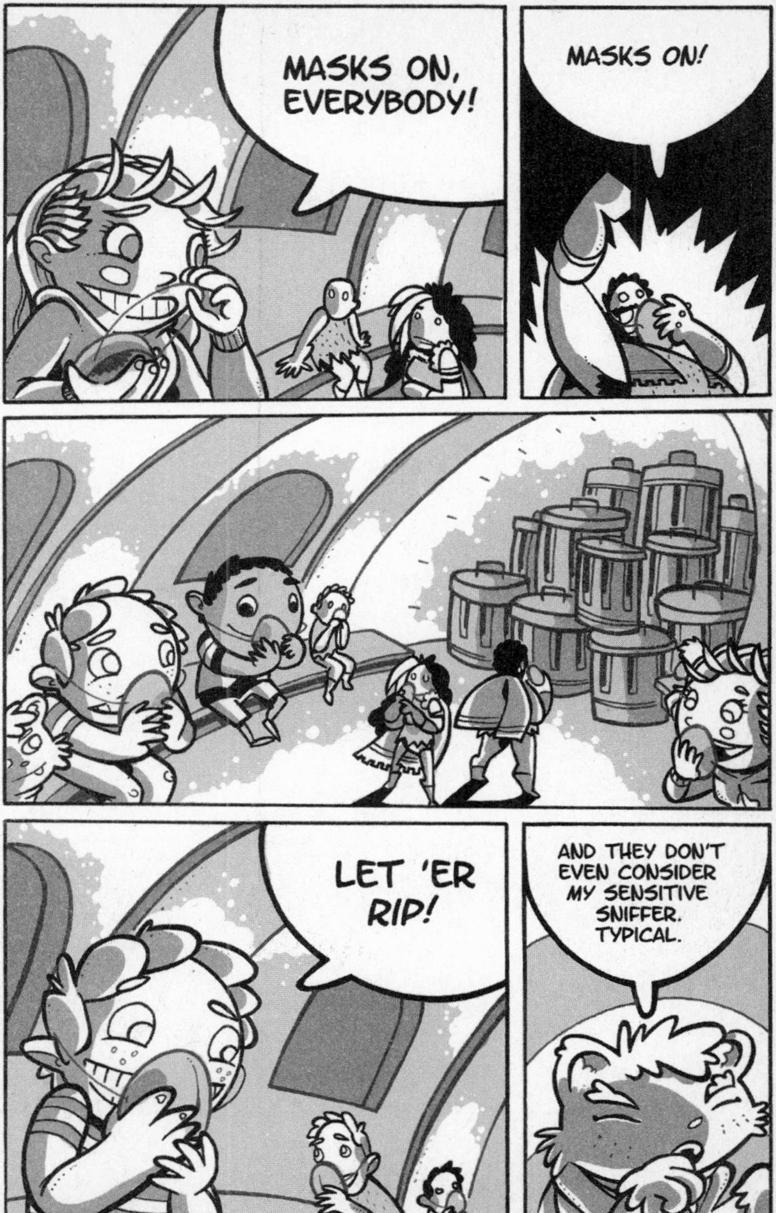
MASKS ON, EVERYBODY!
MASKS ON!
LET 'ER RIP!
AND THEY DON'T EVEN CONSIDER MY SENSITIVE SNIFFER. TYPICAL.

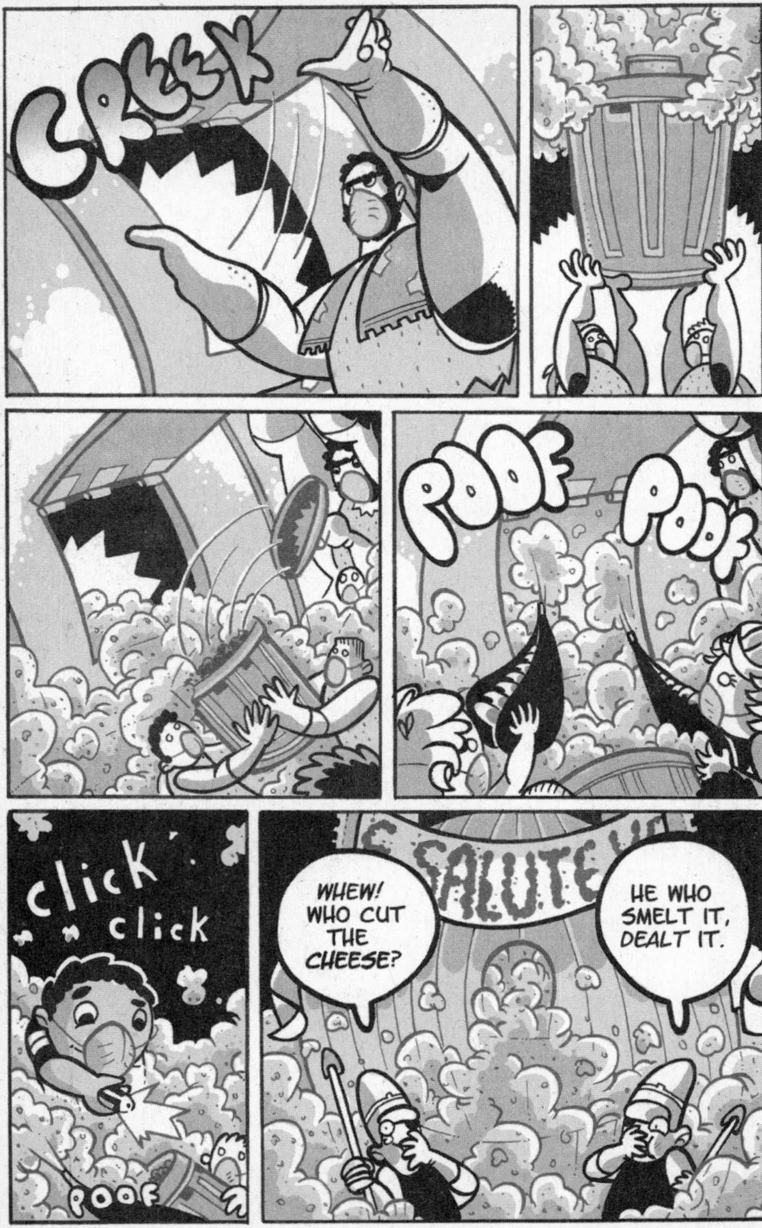
CREEK
POOF
POOF
click
click
POOF
SALUTE
WHEW! WHO CUT THE CHEESE?
HE WHO SMELT IT, DEALT IT.

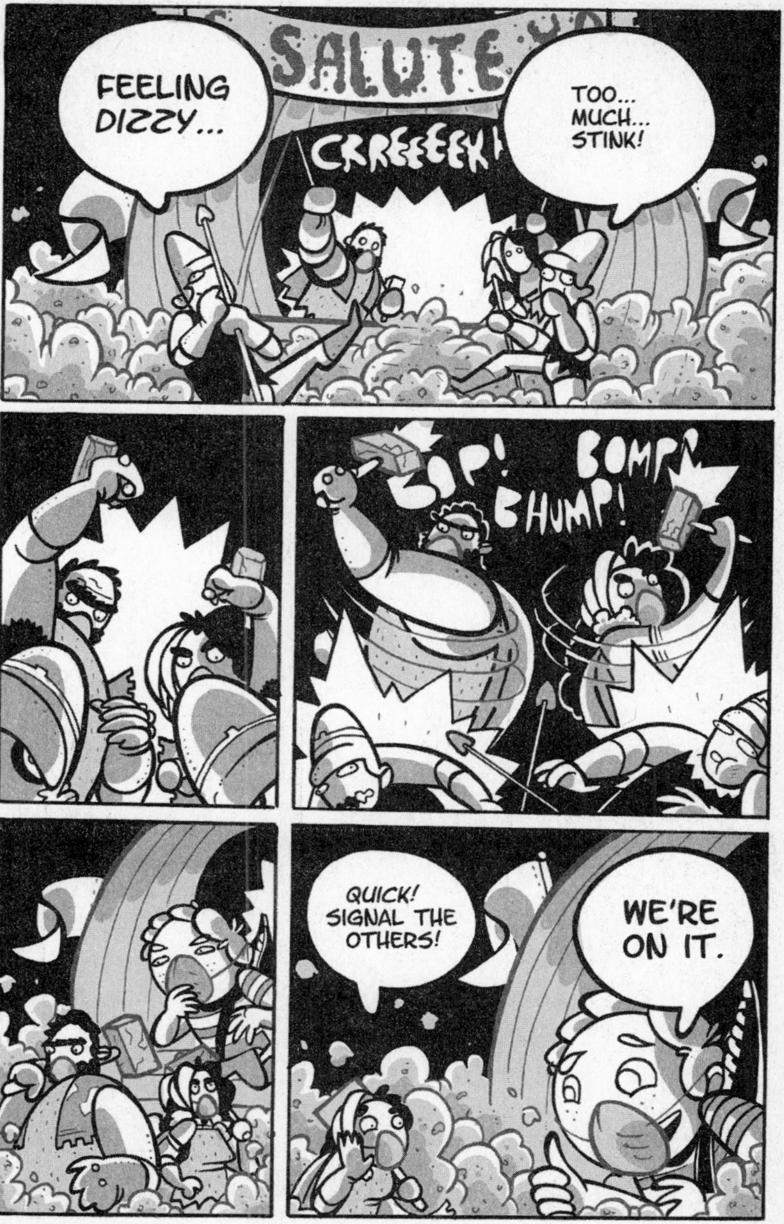
SALUTE
FEELING DIZZY...
CREEEEK!
TOO... MUCH... STINK!
BOMP!
CHUMP!
QUICK! SIGNAL THE OTHERS!
WE'RE ON IT.

WOOSH!

UNGH! AARGH! DESTROY....HUMANS!

UH-OH!

OKAY, STEPH. GAS ME!

PRINCESSES DON'T DO THAT SORT OF THING.

NOT YOUR GAS. *THAT* GAS!

FFWOOOOSHH!!!

FLAME ON!!

UNG!!! FIRE!!

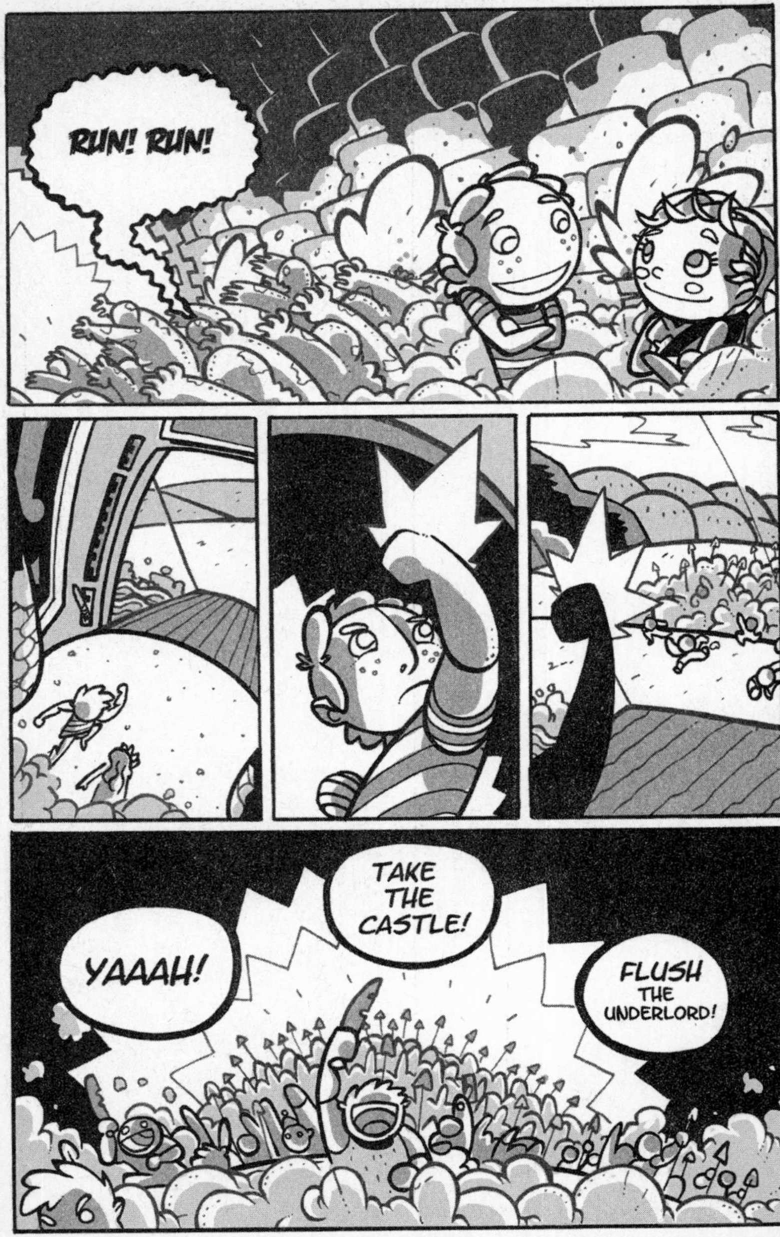
RUN! RUN!
TAKE THE CASTLE!
YAAAH!
FLUSH THE UNDERLORD!

A SHORT FIGHT LATER...

THREE CHEERS FOR THE LOST PRINCE! 'IP, IP...

'URRAH! URRAH!

DON'T FORGET ABOUT THE LOST PRINCESS, AND LOST, UM... HIPPO RIDER?

NOW I'M THINKING CHEESE DETECTOR.

'URRAH! 'URRAH!

WELL DONE, PRINCE. AFTER THIS, TAKIN' PORT 'EINIE SHOULD BE A SNAP!

ONCE YOU GET PAST THE SEA SERPENT.

SEA SERPENT?!

ZEKE, IT'S FIVE THIRTY!

GASP!

CAITLYN! THE STORE OPENING!

GUYS, WE HATE TO STORM AND RUN, BUT...

WAIT, WE ALMOST FORGOT!

WHAT?

WE NEED TO BRING THE SPIES SOMETHING MAGICAL!

SOMETHING MAGICAL? TAKE A DHOW-NAUGHT.

A DOUGH-NUT?

THERE'S NO TIME TO EAT!

NO, A DHOW-NAUGHT-- ONE OF THOSE 'UNGRY ROCKS. THEY'RE ENCHANTED.

WORKS FOR ME. HEY, WHERE'S FITZ?

FITZIE? FITZIE?!

OH, NO. IS HE...?

HIDING OUT LIKE A SENSIBLE CAT? YES, HE IS.

YOU'RE ALL RIGHT!

YES, THAT'S, PRRR, NICE. LOWER... AND KEEP THAT BUG MUNCHER AWAY FROM MY TAIL!

CHOMP

 LET'S *GO!* WE'VE GOT TO MAKE THAT OPENING.

 YOU'RE RIGHT. I HAVE A FEELING SOMETHING WEIRD IS GONNA HAPPEN.

 WEIRDER THAN *THIS?* THAT'S SAYING SOMETHING.

CHAPTER

14

Bad Undies

We pounded up the driveway—about ten minutes late.

Oops.

Caitlyn was pacing outside. Queen Kong in full meltdown mode.

"You little buzz-crushers!" she yelled. "You're in *so* much trouble. Where *were* you?"

"We, uh . . . ," I began.

"Never mind where you were," said Caitlyn. "*Move it!*"

She hustled us over to the waiting limousine.

"But we need to clean up," said Stephanie.

"Get. In. That. Car," Caitlyn growled. "Now!"

I rolled the dhow-naught into the bushes. We got in the car.

Fitz stayed behind. Smart cat.

All the way to Beefy D's store, Caitlyn chewed us out in new and creative ways. Not even Stephanie could slip a word in.

But when we arrived—*bam!* The lights, red carpet, and TV cameras finally stopped Queen Kong's mouth. "Whoa" was all she could say.

The limo door opened, and we stepped out to a cheering crowd. It fell silent like *that.* "Who the heck are *they*?" someone said.

"Guess they've never seen royalty before," Hector muttered.

We shuffled up the carpet to the black building. Overhead an enormous pink sign flashed: BAD UNDIES.

"Do you see that?" I hissed to Steph.

"Yeah," she said.

"Weird," said Hector.

Stephanie shrugged. "Could just be a coincidence."

Inside the huge store, the music thumped so loud, the bass rattled your fillings. Racks and racks of underwear filled the place. Models strolled up and down a stage and runway at the far end.

"Check *them* out," said Hector. "Do they remind you of anyone?"

I looked closer. The models wore their underwear *outside* their clothes, just like the Undies. And just like Beefy D.

Huh.

"Okay, *that's* weird," said Steph.

People crushed around a table piled high with sweets. I spotted Melvin Prang and his parents, along with three kids—probably the other schools' contest winners.

But no Beefy D.

"Where's the bathroom?" Stephanie asked a store employee.

The woman pointed to a corner.

"Me too," I said, joining Steph.

Hector crossed his arms. "I'll scope out the scene, pahangle."

We found the bathrooms in a short hallway off the main floor. Steph entered the *Kitties*, but the *Dawgs'* door was locked. As I waited, I checked out the Beefy D posters. BAD UNDIES: EVIL IS AWESOME, they read.

Then I noticed a third door, slightly ajar. I wandered over.

A voice rose. "I don't *care* if it's not where I saw it. *Find* my *Throne!*"

I peeked through the doorway at a man's broad

back. A very short man.

"Search the whole house," he snarled into his cell phone. "No, they don't. They think I'm a stupid rapper, *padangle.*"

It was Beefy D. My breath caught in my throat. So he wasn't a rapper, but who was he? *Hmm . . .* short, powerful, looking for a throne . . .

Beefy D was the *UnderLord!*

And his bodyguards were searching *our* house.

"Right," said the man. "And pick up that other thing."

He turned suddenly. I found myself face-to-face with the dark lord of Underwhere. And, *boy*, what a face—so ugly, it'd make onions cry.

His eyes widened. The UnderLord passed a hand before his face. In a flash of blue light, Beefy D's pasty skin, average features, and gold teeth were in place.

"Whoa, pahangle!" he said. "You 'most spooked

me outta mah spangle."

I backed up, pointing. "You . . . you," I said.

The UnderLord advanced. "What's the hapangle, mah frangle?"

"Your face." I edged into the hallway.

He leaned closer, teeth glinting and rotten-egg smell reeking. "Whatever ya *think* ya peeped, they'll never believe ya."

I opened my mouth to say who-knows-what. Just then, Stephanie left the *Kitties* room, and two women stepped into the hall behind me.

"*There* you are, you naughty rap god, you," said the taller one. She was a breathless brunette with big eyes. "We've been searching everywhere. It's showtime!"

"Let's go, you adorable podrangle," said the shorter, blonder one.

The UnderLord stepped close to Steph and me. "Mah public awaits. *Pardonnez*-mangle." His grin looked like the grille of a fancy sports car.

The women linked arms, leading Beefy D to the stage. He flashed peace signs and blew kisses to the crowd.

We followed at a safe distance.

"He's the UnderLord for sure," I told Steph.

"You have proof?" she said.

"I saw his *real* face—seriously ugly—before he changed it to the Beefy D face. And his guys are searching our house for the throne."

"But why would the UnderLord pretend to be a *rapper*?" she asked.

I shook my head. "I don't know. He's a music lover?"

Steph's jaw tightened. "We've got to expose that phony."

"But how?"

Beefy D was welcoming the group. "Yo, yo, yo! How's the foodangle?"

"Evil!" the crowd called.

"And what kind of undies do ya like?"

"Bad!" everyone chanted.

"So right!" said Beefy D.

"So right!" they echoed.

Hector joined us. "Wow," he said. "I bet he could make them do anything right now."

That's when it hit me.

"Of course!" I said, turning to face them both. "*That's* why the UnderLord's a rapper. Think about it. Who can affect lots of people? Who can set trends, mold minds, and make a ton of money at it?"

"A politician?" asked Hector.

"A rapper," said Steph.

"So how do we unwrap this phony?" I said.

Beefy D called the contest winners up. The kids stood awkwardly beside him—except Melvin, who raised a fist and shouted, "Yo, yo, yo!"

I wished I'd never written that stupid rap for him.

Hmm . . . stupid rap. Now *that* was an idea.

"Rap for us, Beefy!" I shouted.

Hector caught on. "Yeah, we want *rap*! We want *rap*!"

The people near us took up the chant, and soon the whole crowd got into it.

The tall brunette shook her head. "I don't think . . ."

"Uh, I'm missin' mah posse, mah bandangle." Beefy D glanced nervously around. "Can't rap without 'em."

"Awww," the group whined.

"Pleeease," said a pretty lady near the stage.

"Didn't bring mah music," said Beefy D. He glanced back at the DJ, who shook her head. "Sorry, mah frangles."

The pretty woman wouldn't give up. "You could rap *freestyle*. We'll clap the beat." She put her hands together. Soon the whole house picked up the rhythm.

The fake rapper gave a shaky smile. He was stuck, and he knew it. "A'right, a'right, mah padangles. Lemme lay this down for ya."

Name is Beefy D,
I don't come from good family.
And the frangle of mah drangle is
an elephant strangle.
West coast, east coast,
All your coasts I'm gonna roast
'Cuz I come from down under.
Under where? Under there!
Pardon me, padangle, while ah
shake mah derriere!

And then Beefy D broke into one of the lamest dances I've ever seen. It looked like angry wasps had slipped into his oversized pants and were stinging him everywhere. His rapping and dancing were so far off the beat, he'd have had to take a train to get back to it.

I looked around. Mouths hung open. A few people made faces like they smelled something bad.

And that something was Beefy D.

He didn't notice. Carried away with his bad self, the rapper hopped offstage and danced in the audience. This was my chance.

Before I could lose my nerve, I nudged Hector and Steph. "Let's go!"

We dashed for the stage and pounded up the steps. I grabbed the mike.

"Listen to me!" I said. "This guy's no rapper. Check it out!"

Hector made beat-box sounds, and I chanted the rhyme I'd written for Melvin:

Zombies in the evening,
Zombies in the morning,
Zombies in your underwear,
They never give a warning.
Creeping through your kitchen,
Don't you dare to linger,
Hiding in your breakfast—
Whoops! I found a finger!

The crowd stomped and clapped. "Go, kid, go!" someone shouted.

When I reached the end, the audience hooted and hollered. Smiles covered everyone's faces, everyone's except Beefy D's and Melvin's.

"See? He's not really a rapper!" I yelled over the applause. "Even *I* can out-rap him."

"So can my dog!" someone shouted. People laughed.

I raised my hand. "No, you don't get it. He's

the *UnderLord*. He's come to conquer our world!"

"That's a lie-angle! I'm Beefy D! The best!" cried the bogus rapper.

The crowd hooted. "You mean the *lamest*!" a chunky woman yelled. "That kid out-rapped you, no contest."

Beefy D's face turned the color of a blood orange. "*That's*—," he choked out. Then he recovered some control. "Uh, ya got things all skimble-skamble, padangles. Beefy D be the baddest rapper around."

"Sure you are," said a tall redheaded man, "if bad means *bad*."

Beefy D ground his teeth. "Don't get the Beefster riled—"

Steph took the mike. "Zeke's telling the truth!" she said. "The UnderLord has enslaved one world, and now he wants ours. He's evil!"

"Don't listen to those nitwits!" cried the

UnderLord, his Beefy accent slipping. "Are all you Uplanders *morons*?"

"Who you callin' a moron, *shrimp*?" The heavy woman waded toward him, swinging her purse. The mob surrounded them. I lost sight of the UnderLord.

"You had to go and ruin it, runt," said a voice behind me.

I spun. Melvin stood there, fists clenched.

Uh-oh.

"Not now, Melvin," I said.

"My first time onstage, and you blew it for me."

Steph and Hector stood shoulder to shoulder with me. "Hey, Mel," she said. "The TV reporter wants to interview you."

"Me?" Melvin brightened. Then he glared at me. "This isn't over, midget. Wait and see." He hurried off.

"Did the TV guys really want him?" I asked.

"Sure," said Hector. "For the new reality show, *Who Wants to Be a Dorkus?*"

I scanned the crowd. "Hey, where's the UnderLord?"

"I don't know," said Steph. "But we better go before Melvin gets back."

On the way out, we searched the packed store, but couldn't spot the fake rapper. Too much confusion. The little man had vanished like a rat down a hole. We met Caitlyn outside.

"Call me psychic," said Hector, "but I have a feeling that we won't be riding home in Beefy D's limo."

And what do you know? The Amazing Hectorini was right.

CHAPTER
15

Science Stinks

After all that excitement, the next day was a let-down. The UnderLord had escaped, and who knew what he'd try next, or where? The H.U.S.H. agents liked their dhow-naught, but they didn't believe us when we told them that the UnderLord had been Beefy D.

And Caitlyn wouldn't speak to us because she was so embarrassed.

(Well, at least there was *one* bright spot.)

But all that was overshadowed by something

even more depressing: schoolwork.

Just before our break, Mrs. Ricotta announced, "When we come back, everyone will present their science projects."

Sheesh. I was doomed.

At recess, I slumped on the jungle gym. "I'm going to flunk science," I told Hector. "In all the excitement, I sort of forgot to redo my experiment."

"That's what happens when you put saving Undies before schoolwork," said Steph.

I hated to admit it, but she was right.

Hector smiled. "I *should* let you suffer longer, but I'm just too great a guy."

"What do you mean?" I said.

"Don't you see? We captured that castle because you understood the science of making methane."

"Hey, that's right!" I said.

"You *are* good with gas," said Stephanie.

I shook my head. "Yeah, but Mrs. Ricotta doesn't know that. Too bad I can't use our castle attack as my science project."

Hector reached into his book bag. He pulled out some blown-up photos. "As a matter of fact," he said, "you can."

When my turn came, I got more scientific than Dr. Science. I covered the blackboard with diagrams showing how to make methane gas with a rotten banana.

"This was my project," I said, "until a clumsy cat broke the jar."

"That's no excuse," said Mrs. Ricotta. "Everyone must show results."

I grinned. "Oh, I will. You see, the broken jar released lots of stinky gas—"

"Just like your armpits!" shouted Melvin Prang.

The class giggled.

"Settle down!" said the teacher. "Continue, Zeke."

I paced. "And that got me thinking about methane. I mean, how do we use it? My research showed that ancient people used it in warfare."

"Is that so?" said Mrs. Ricotta.

"Uh-huh," I said. (It wasn't really.) "So I tried to re-create how a methane attack might have gone."

I displayed a photo. It showed the oversized garbage jars from Skivvy Town. "First, you'd need to make a *lot* of gas. Like this."

"Like *you*," said Melvin.

Mrs. Ricotta glared. "Melvin, I'm warning you."

"Then, you'd need to find a way of moving that gas. . . ." I showed the photo of Steph and me working the bellows.

"Like—," Melvin began.

"Melvin, go sit outside!" Mrs. Ricotta watched

him leave, then turned back to me. "Zeke, that's very impressive—A-quality work."

I beamed. It *was* A-quality work, and *I* had done it.

"And finally," I said, "you'd need to sneak all of this into a city—in a kind of Trojan Buns."

"Zeke!" said our teacher.

Up went the pictures of the attack. Everyone hooted and clapped when I explained how we had launched the gas.

"And this attack would succeed?" asked Stephanie's friend Heather.

"It *did*," I said triumphantly. "Uh, I mean . . . yeah, it would."

Mrs. Ricotta frowned. "*Hmph.* C-minus."

"A C-*minus*?!" I said. "What about the A-quality work?"

She gave me a long look over her glasses. "Although your science was sound, the way you

162

used it was not."

"But—"

"I am disappointed that you have once again stooped to potty humor. Really, Zeke, it's beneath you."

I had the perfect comeback to that. But I just bit my lip. Sometimes, you've got to quit while you're ahead.

The rest of the day passed quietly. Melvin Prang didn't cream me; I guessed he was watching and waiting.

After school, I cruised home with Stephanie and Hector.

"What next?" asked Hector.

"I was thinking snacks," I said.

Steph elbowed me. "He was talking about Underwhere."

"I knew that," I said. We turned onto our street.

"What do *you* think about Underwhere?"

"Well, they *do* seem to need our help," she said. "And the UnderLord still—"

A furry body shot from the bushes and scaled me like a tree. "Ow! Those claws *hurt*." It was Fitz.

"Meer, murr," he said, climbing into my arms. "Meer murr *reoww*!"

"Something's up," said Hector.

"Yeah," I said. I freed Fitz's claws from my shirt. "Your cat's up *me*."

Just then, a tall, snowy-haired man hurried down our driveway. He looked like a stork in a high wind—all ruffled feathers and skinny legs.

"Are you Zeke and Stephanie?" he asked.

"Yes . . . ?" said Steph.

"Great milk of Minerva!" said the man. "You must come with me right away."

"Uh, not to be rude," I said, "but who the heck are you?"

The stork man blinked. "We spoke. I'm Dr. J. Robert Prufrock, your Great-aunt Zenobia's friend."

"Mrrow," said Fitz.

"What's this about?" said Hector.

Dr. Prufrock ran a hand through his hair, making it stand straight up.

"No time to explain," he said. "My artifact is missing, and I'm afraid the UnderLord may have taken it. I need your help right away."

I looked at the cat. "Well, meow muffin," I said. "Here we go again."

Fitz rolled his eyes. "Mwwrr."

Avast, ye tighty-whities!

Turn the page for a peek at the
arrrgh-inspiring second Underwhere adventure!

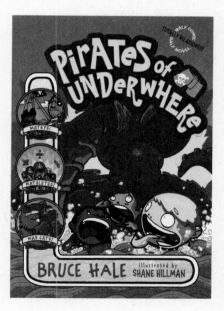

PiRATES of UNDERWHERE

"I last saw it here, in the library."

We peeked into a room. Books lined the walls and rose from the floor in piles like ruined towers. A sea of papers lapped around them. Crusty dishes and coffee mugs sat everywhere—some with flies, some without. Rumpled clothes, empty shoe boxes, three chessboards, a stuffed anaconda, and a full suit of rusty armor completed the picture.

"Um, Dr. Prufrock?" I said.

"Yes, Stephanie?"

"Are you sure you haven't just *misplaced* your artifact?"

He frowned and looked about. "Er . . . well, yes, pretty sure."

Zeke put his hands on his hips. "So . . . what are we looking for?"

"Well," said Dr. Prufrock, "the artifact looks rather like a common toilet brush."

Hector and Zeke snickered. I could have predicted that.

"Only it's larger and painted with colorful runes," said the doctor.

Hector gazed out the window. "Has it also got golden bristles?" he asked.

"Yes," said Dr. Prufrock.

"And is it about *so* long?" Hector held his hands apart.

"Why, yes."

"With some kind of sparkly ring around the handle?"

"That's it exactly!" said the doctor. "Do you see it?"

Hector pointed outside. "Sure, it's in that cat's mouth!"